THE
DollarFly Girls

TODD H. DAVIS

A JENSEN SIBLINGS TANGENT

Todd H. Davis

The DollarFly Girls
Copyright © 2022 by Todd H. Davis

Name: Davis, Todd H. (1963)
Title: The DollarFly Girls / Todd H. Davis
Series: The Jensen Siblings: book 4
Summary: "Teenager Alia recounts her experience and the people she
            met while she was held captive in a suburban sex trafficking
            ring. No graphic details." – Author.

ISBN: 978-1-7373413-6-9 paperback
            978-1-7373413-7-6 hardcover

Subject: Sexual abuse; [BISAC: | **FICTION** / Literary | **FICTION** /
            Psychological | **FICTION** / Thrillers / Psychological |
            FICTION / Thrillers / Suspense]

Rev. 1

Independently published, Cypress, Texas, USA
For information, contact www.toddhdavis.com

Cover photo by Anna Malysheva
Cover design by Todd H. Davis

THE

DOLLARFLY GIRLS

A novel

Books by Todd H. Davis

The Trailer Behind the Garage

The Gas Station Girl

The Lingering Scent of Wrong Assumptions

The DollarFly Girls

Author's Note

All too often, facts are scarier than fiction. On April 8, 2022, a fifteen-year-old girl walked out of a Dallas Mavericks basketball game at the American Airlines Center after telling her father that she was going to the restroom. Surveillance video showed her walking out of the arena with an unknown person and disappearing into a nearby parking garage. She did not appear to leave by force.

Unhappy with the police response, her parents contacted the Texas Counter-Trafficking Initiative, a non-profit organization dedicated to assisting families and law enforcement agencies in locating juvenile victims of commercial sexual exploitation. Its investigators used facial recognition software to find the girl's photos posted to a prostitution website with information indicating she was likely in Oklahoma City.

Based on the information gleaned from the website, Oklahoma City police raided a hotel near the airport and arrested three for sex trafficking. However, they did not find the girl.

On April 18, ten days after she disappeared, Oklahoma City police found her with help from an anonymous tip. They arrested and charged five more people, bringing the total number of people charged in her abduction and sex trafficking to eight. Six of those were women.

Todd H. Davis

The Assignment

The chocolate-colored Labrador Retriever stood in the front hallway, facing the door, waiting for his human mother to come and open it. He had already barked to get her attention in case she didn't hear the doorbell. He barked a reminder just as she rounded the corner. His tail wagged faster at her appearance.

"I heard you the first time," she scolded, patting his head before reaching for the door handle.

"Hi, Ms. Amanda," the young woman at the entrance said as Amanda Butler opened the door wider. "Hi, Bob Barker," she added, patting the dog's head as he came out to sniff her legs.

Amanda stepped aside to make room for the girl. "Come on in, Alia. Are you here for a cuddle session with Bob Barker or just to take him for a walk?"

The older teenager lived three houses down with Amanda's son Ty and his wife Sophie, and Sophie's younger siblings, John and Emi. Alia originally began taking the Butlers' dog for walks when she first came to live with Ty and Sophie a year and a half earlier. The dog walking started as something to ease her boredom but quickly evolved into a sort of therapy on stressful days. Doggie cuddles always cheered her up.

"Today I came to talk to you."

Amanda hugged Alia before leading her to the living room. "Can I get you a lemonade or Coke or something?"

"You got anything harder?"

"Oh. That serious, huh?" Amanda looked at her for a moment to assess her mental state. No red nose or eyes or smeared mascara. Maybe just a hard day at school. "Sorry, no alcohol for you," she said with a smile. "I can't contribute to the delinquency of a minor. Oh. But you're not a minor, are you?"

"Not for a while now. Nineteen's in that in-between stage where I'm an adult, but not adult enough. And you're too late to save me from delinquency. I've been a delinquent for a couple of years now."

"Stop it. Have a seat on the sofa and I'll get you lemonade."

Alia sat on the end of the sofa closest to the loveseat that was positioned at a right angle to it. Bob Barker hopped up onto the sofa next to her and put his head in her lap. He was determined to provide cuddle therapy whether Alia wanted it or not.

The Butler home is comfortable, Alia thought. She'd visited many times with the excuse of taking the dog for a walk and then staying to chat. She had even spent one Christmas night with them when her host family – as a friend called Ty, Sophie, and Sophie's siblings, as if Alia was an exchange student – went out of town to visit Sophie's grandmother. *Host family* was the best term Alia could think of regarding their arrangement. Which would make Amanda and Henry what? Host-in-laws?

Amanda returned to the living room with two glasses of lemonade. After handing one to Alia, she plopped herself down on the loveseat. "So, what's up?"

Alia pulled a folded sheet of paper from a back pocket and opened it up. "It's nothing serious. I just need help deciding how to do a school assignment." She handed the paper to Ms. Amanda.

"You live with a family of geniuses. At least from the Jensen side. My son's talent is in other areas. Have you asked them?" She began reading Alia's paper before waiting for an answer.

Teacher: Mrs. Woods
Class: Sociology
Assignment: Since we recently covered significant events that impacted society, culture, or country, I want you to write about something of a more personal nature that had an impact on your life. It must be at least 5 pages, double-spaced. More pages are fine, but I might not be able to read it all. Examples include, but are not limited to, moving to a new city or neighborhood, the death of a loved one, adoption (self or sibling), a serious medical condition of a family member, and winning the lottery.
Objective: Describe the event's impact on you. You decide how many or how few details to provide about the impactful event itself.

"I think Ty would probably have good advice for this. But he doesn't get home until around six. No one's home yet," Alia explained. "Sophie's still at school and John and Emi are with friends. So, I came here. Besides I thought someone with more life experience would have better advice."

"That's a polite way of calling me old."

Alia tried to think of a response when Amanda rattled the paper. "I don't think you need help finding something that impacted your life. You have several to choose from. Certainly not anything worthy of a hard drink."

"That's just it. I don't like talking about my old life before I got here. I'm already self-conscious enough without having people know all my… uh… dirt."

"What about that thing with your father last year? People already know about that."

"Yeah, but if I write about that, then I have to explain why I live with Ty and Sophie and not with my parents. And that just brings up all that other stuff."

"Do you have to present this in front of the class?"

"No. It's just a paper to turn in to the teacher."

"That doesn't seem so bad. Don't you trust your teacher to keep it confidential?"

"Well…uh… yeah, I guess."

Amanda took a sip of lemonade and watched for a moment as Alia stroked Bob Barker's fur.

"Is this more about dredging up bad memories than about deciding which topic to write about?" Amanda asked.

Alia leaned down to put her face close to the dog. The retriever raised his head and licked her cheek.

"Yes. I guess I'm trying to avoid it."

That may be worthy of hard liquor, Amanda thought. "I think the brain tries to hold on to bad memories that you haven't fully reconciled. They're like unfinished business that the brain keeps around, waiting for you to complete. But if you put all those memories on paper – or the computer – then you relieve your brain of the responsibility of holding onto them. So, writing it down may help you in the long run."

Alia pressed her lips together and scrunched up one side of her face.

"You think I'm just blowing smoke, don't you?" Amanda asked rhetorically.

Alia shrugged.

"Whether I write it down or not, I'll never forget my time with Lauren and Bulldog and the girls."

"I only have a general idea of what you went through and I'm sure you'll never forget it. But the details might fade."

Alia opened her mouth and inhaled deeply, about to protest. *You have no idea what I went through and no idea how impossible it is to forget.* But she closed her mouth and kept those thoughts to herself. It wasn't fair to judge Ms. Amanda on something she didn't know.

"When I was in high school, I had a falling out with my best friend," Amanda said. "At my last high school reunion, she was there, and I was still resentful. And you know what?" she asked, raising her eyebrows.

Alia took that as a cue to respond. She shook her head.

"I couldn't remember why," Amanda said. "I still don't remember. I was mad at her for years over something I can't remember."

"I don't think this is the same thing. I'll remember this for a long time."

Amanda nodded as if acknowledging her own ignorance of Alia's life. "You know you best. I just know that emotional scars hang around long after you forget the details," Amanda continued. "You'll just remember that it was something significant at the time." She held up the assignment paper. "Or impactful, as your teacher says."

"Like why I get nervous when I see a white Infiniti SUV."

"You do? Why? No. Don't tell me. Write it all down. Everything. Including the white SUV. I'll proof the paper for you before you turn it in."

Alia sighed heavily, which made Bob Barker look up. *Maybe it wouldn't be a bad idea for someone else to understand what I went through. Someone I trust, like Ms. Amanda.*

Bob Barker raised himself on his front paws and licked her face again.

"Can I take Bob Barker for a walk?"

"Sure. You know where the leash is."

Alia rose from the sofa and the dog eagerly jumped off and stood beside her, looking up expectantly.

"Alia."

Alia turned to look at Amanda.

"Enjoy this life. Prom's coming up. Then graduation. Then our vacation to celebrate all you graduates. It's hard to believe we have three in one family. You, Anna, and John. Everyone's growing up."

"Yes, ma'am." She smiled at the warmth of Amanda's statement. Anna was her daughter, soon to graduate from college, and John was Ty's brother-in-law, graduating with Alia from Cypress Grove High School. Alia had no direct relation to the Butlers, yet Amanda counted her as part of the family.

"Give me a hug before you walk out," Amanda ordered. "And don't let the past get in the way of the present."

My First Life

I wasn't a good daughter. That would be my sister Alma. She's five years older than me and did whatever my parents asked, even if she didn't want to. I was the opposite. If something didn't make sense to me, I tried to get out of it.

My father arranged for Alma to get married when she was twenty. They picked out a nice young man for her. Someone from Syria, my parent's country, from their culture. From a family that my relatives knew very well. He just wasn't someone Alma knew very well. She had a few bouts of crying before the wedding to a man she barely knew. And a few bouts of crying after. But only when my father wasn't around. The arrangement was mostly his idea. My mother just went along as she usually does.

An arranged marriage was going to be my fate, too, when I finished high school. If I wanted to go to college, I could do so as a married woman, and only if my husband agreed to it. I thought getting married at twenty was much too young, especially to someone you barely know. Funny, because I now live with John Jensen's family. And the head of the family is his sister Sophie and his brother-in-law, Ty. And Sophie got married when she was nineteen. *But…* she knew Ty for several years, and John said she was the one who pushed for an early wedding.

I didn't want to get married that young and I didn't want to get married to someone I didn't know. I didn't want to do a lot of things my parents wanted me to do, like dressing the way they wanted, avoiding certain foods, and avoiding anything that looked fun. My parents said it was our culture. But that's not right. It was *their* culture. They still think of themselves as Syrian. I was born in St. Louis. My culture is American culture.

Since I was nine, I had to wear long-sleeve blouses. I had to wear long pants or leggings, even if I wore a dress. I had to cover my head when I left the house. Once, when I was outside playing – maybe eleven years old – my hijab slipped off and I didn't fix it. My father saw it and grabbed me by my hair and dragged me back to the house. After beating my butt, he cut my hair off. Not bald, just ugly. I cried and my mom raised her voice at him for doing such an extreme punishment. He slapped her so hard that she fell against the cabinet and busted her chin. She had to get stitches. I never heard her raise her voice to him again.

After that, I made sure I looked right when my parents or their friends were around. But when I went to school, I took the hijab off. Sometimes I pushed my sleeves up. When I went to my friends' houses, I would try on their clothes. Their shorts and tank tops and skirts.

The summer between tenth and eleventh grade I snuck out to a pool party and wore a friend's one-piece swimsuit. My parents thought I was at a different friend's house. That's where I met Connor. I'd seen him at school but hadn't talked to him.

But we talked that day. He put me on his shoulders in the pool. I literally had my legs around his neck. My bare legs. My mother would've had a heart attack if she'd found out. My dad would have beat the crap out of me. It didn't take much to set him off. Any act of disobedience was disrespectful to him, our heritage, and our god. I think my father suspected I was doing things he didn't approve but he didn't catch me. Mostly, he was irritated by my constant questioning of his beliefs. "Why can't I dress like my friends?" "Why can't we eat what my friends eat?" His answers usually didn't make sense to me, so I didn't feel compelled to follow dumb rules that he couldn't even explain. At least, I didn't feel compelled to obey when I was away from him. But if I was caught breaking them, there would be serious consequences. At the time I thought a god must only be as powerful as its followers are obedient.

When I was sixteen, shortly before my junior year, my father announced he had found a suitable husband for me. A friend of a cousin. The boy lived in Syria, of course. After high school, the plan was for us to go to Syria for the wedding, and the guy would come back with me as my husband. Maybe it would happen when I was nineteen or twenty. The boy's parents would help my father set up a grocery store. By help, I mean they would give my father money he would use for the store. He was basically selling me.

I liked Connor. I enjoyed spending time with him. We would go in groups to the mall or a movie and I would always sit by him. And we would hold hands. I don't think I was in love. I think it was the thrill of being sneaky. But after my father told me about my arranged marriage, I could only think about Connor. So, I kissed him right in front of our friends. A couple of weeks later, I told my parents I had a project meeting after school and would be home late. But I really went to Connor's house. And no one else was home. Even if my dad forced me to marry some guy I didn't know, at least I got to choose who to give my virginity to.

Not long after that, I got into an argument with my parents – one of many – which somehow got into the subject of how women should behave around their husbands, which somehow got into what my fiancé would expect of me, which somehow got into how a girl should retain her purity for her husband. The more they talked, the angrier I got. It's my life, not theirs. In a fit of anger, I let them know I was no longer a virgin. Actually, I wanted them to know, but I just hadn't planned on telling them at that moment. I hoped that would be enough reason to call off the marriage. My father would have to get his money another way.

Sometimes when I get super angry, I forget about the consequences. This was one of those times. I had just confessed that I dishonored the family. That has consequences. My father's handprint on my face disappeared by the next day. It was a few more days for the bruises and welts on my backside to disappear. Sitting in school was difficult that week. My biggest fear about getting married to a stranger from my father's country is that he would be like my father. And the thought of spending my life with someone like that makes me want to puke.

I was on Instagram. I had been for a couple of years, but my parents didn't know. They forbid me from using social media. But how can any modern person get by without it? I didn't make it private, but only a few close friends had my account. Still, I didn't use my real name so my parents or their friends wouldn't find it.

I posted pics and also ranted about my life. I had already ranted about the marriage arrangement. That's one reason I didn't give Connor my Instagram. Between my pics of secretly wearing my friends' clothes, I ranted. Strict parents. Stupid rules. A future of misery with some stranger I'm supposed to marry. People would leave comments with sympathy, which made me feel a little better. Not much, but a little. After the beating for losing my virginity, I posted pics of my face and the backs of my thighs. And I ranted.

On one of my earlier photo rant posts, a guy Direct Messaged me. @bulldog82. He was sympathetic. We chatted casually. Nothing serious. After the epic rant, he DM'd me again. He told me what I was going through wasn't right. Parents shouldn't treat their kids like that. If I needed a place to stay, he could help. Of course, I looked up his account. He didn't look like a creepy old man. He looked young. His account included photos of him with other people. At restaurants. At a lake. At a park. Smiling people. It looked like the life I wanted but couldn't have. He said he was from Texas but that he had friends in Missouri who could help. He could even come if I wanted. I passed on that but kept chatting with him.

Then Connor started avoiding me. When I confronted him on it, he said our cultural differences were too much; that it wouldn't work out. What cultural differences? I'm from St. Louis, the same as him. I had already been removing my head covering at school and around my friends. I ate what they ate. Usually. I still couldn't bring myself to eat pork since my parents drilled into me how dirty pigs were. But cheese pizza, pasta, hamburgers, and fries: no problem. I didn't understand what cultural differences he was talking about. But no use; he stopped responding to my texts and chats; wouldn't answer the phone. He was effectively out of my life, and I felt more alone than ever.

Running Away

I poured out my soul to @bulldog82. He told me again that if I needed to get out of there, just let him know and he would make it happen. I thanked him, but this time I didn't say no. Later I heard my parents talking. I can't remember my father's exact words, but it was something about one of his friends finding out who the boy was and talking to him. I assumed "the boy" was Connor and that my father's friend told him that I was engaged. My marriage was still on, but my "sales price" was reduced. Connor was right about a big cultural difference. Compelled marriage is significant.

I ranted again to @bulldog82. He offered once more to help me leave. This time he said he was housesitting for a friend a couple of hours from St. Louis. He could meet me somewhere. When I heard my father yell at my mother again for some petty issue, I decided to accept @bulldog82's offer. He suggested meeting at a shopping mall, and I told him The Galleria is a good place. It wasn't necessarily the closest mall to my house, but it was the easiest to get to by bus. We arranged to meet at the entrance between Macy's and Nordstrom. I stuffed my backpack with toiletries, clothes, and the little stuffed penguin that my friend Elena gave me. It was probably not the most prudent item to pack; it was only about eight inches tall, but I could have fit an extra shirt or more underwear in its place. But the penguin made me smile because it reminded me of Elena's family, the kind of family I wanted. They laugh together and she adores her dad.

Doug – aka @bulldog82 – arrived at the mall entrance with a dog. That was the plan. Look for the guy with a small dog that likes to lick. Doug looked like his pictures. I walked closer and Doug looked at me and smiled. I could tell he recognized me. When I stepped closer, the dog wagged its tail and pulled at the leash to come to me. It was not chihuahua-small, but medium-sized. It looked like my neighbor's Australian Shepherd. When I got even closer, the dog stood on its hind legs and put its paws on my legs.

Doug pulled the dog back and said, "Down, Diamond." Then he squatted down next to the dog and scratched it behind its ears.

"Do you like ice cream, @MindOfHerOwn148?" Those were Doug's first words to me in person, using my Instagram handle. *Do I like ice cream?*

I nodded. "Yeah," I managed to say, feeling awkward at meeting someone for the first time in person. "My real name's Alia."

"My real-life name is Doug, but my friends call me Bulldog. Since we have a dog with us, we have to go to a place where we can sit outside."

I merely replied, "Okay."

He held the leash out for me to take. "Diamond likes you."

I took the leash and patted the dog's head.

"Come on, let's go get ice cream," Doug said.

He started walking to the parking lot. Diamond started walking towards Doug and I just followed, holding the leash. Doug led the way to a white Dodge Challenger. He put the dog in the back seat with my backpack, but once I was seated, Diamond climbed into the front and sat in my lap.

"She rode in that seat on the way here. I guess she thinks it's hers," Doug joked. "Are you okay with that?"

I didn't mind having Diamond sit in my lap. Somehow, things seemed less awkward with a dog.

In the car, Doug asked about the latest blowup with my father. I talked about my father and about my suspicion of why Connor dumped me. Doug asked what I thought would happen if I stayed.

As I thought about the next three or four years under my father's rule, followed by a loveless marriage to a stranger, my anger rose. Various scenarios ran through my head, all resulting in a bleak future. I had already told Doug some of it through DM, but I gave more details, more of my thoughts, in person. I surprised myself at being able to talk to him so freely. It usually takes me a while to warm up to someone. Maybe it was the dog. Doug was sympathetic.

He said, "My friends and I have helped others in trouble. People with no hope for a future and nowhere to go."

We continued the conversation at a patio table outside an ice cream shop. It felt like a date.

"How old are you?" I asked.

He smiled before answering, "I don't want to say, because you'll think I'm too young to help."

He told me he came from a broken family and started working at a young age doing odd jobs. He also told me he and some friends owned rental properties and he helped a friend with her modeling business, lining up clients and setting appointments.

"We're not rich, but it's a decent living. Enough to pay the bills and still have some left over to help someone in need."

Doug gave the last bit of his ice cream to Diamond. She liked it a lot.

After we had finished our ice cream, it was time to decide. Should I leave with Doug or return home? An unknown future or a future of despair. If I went home now, I knew I would get in trouble for going to the mall without telling anyone. Not that they would have let me go if I asked. It almost seemed like less of a risk to go with Doug. That was my decision: go with Doug. He took my phone, set it to airplane mode, then turned it off and put it in the center console of the car; I never saw it again.

We drove to a farm outside of Rolla, where he was staying in a cute little cabin next to a farmhouse. The dog belonged to the family in the farmhouse. Apparently, Diamond got to wander freely around the property. The cabin was a one-bedroom place decorated with scenic prints on the walls, colorful cushions on the dining chairs, and coordinated pillows on the sofa.

That evening, we drove into Rolla for dinner. It felt like another date. After dinner, we went back to the cabin and watched a movie on the TV. It didn't have cable or streaming service or anything. But there was an old-fashioned DVD player with a box of old movies on the floor next to the TV. We watched the animated version of Disney's *The Little Mermaid*. I remember it because I identified with Ariel, rebelling against a controlling father with anger issues who wanted to force her into a life she didn't want.

I wondered if Doug was my Prince Eric. He was charming and confident and gave me hope for a better life. While watching the movie, we drank wine – my first alcohol – and ate popcorn. He put his arm around me on the sofa while we watched and occasionally threw popcorn in my face. And I threw some back.

After the movie, we took turns in the bathroom. When it was Doug's turn to shower, he left the bathroom door open to make it easier to talk. I admit that I snuck a peek through the doorway, but I couldn't see anything through the shower curtain.

That night Doug slept on the couch, and I got the bedroom. He kissed me good night. It was quick, but it was on the lips. I had to think about it for a while before I admitted to myself that I liked it.

The next day, we drove to Tulsa and went shopping for clothes. The kind I couldn't own before. The summer items – running shorts and short-sleeve blouses and mini dresses – were out of season and on clearance. He helped me pick out items, saying things like, "This would look good on you" and "I don't know if you should have this; it'll just make guys stare. But you can try it on if you want." It's supposed to be shameful to wear things that made guys stare, but it was exciting to try them on. I thought we were just window shopping for entertainment because I didn't have enough money to buy all the clothes I tried on. But I couldn't believe Doug insisted on paying for everything. We had a nice dinner and Doug stopped to buy a bottle of wine on the way back to the hotel.

In the hotel room, he encouraged me to model the clothes I'd bought that afternoon, even though he'd already seen me in some of them at the store. He waited in the desk chair each time I went to the bathroom to change outfits. And each time I came out, he complimented me. Even for the T-shirt and running shorts. "Looks good." "Beautiful." "Gorgeous." "I was right. Guys will stare. We'd better take it back." And my favorite comment: "It makes a pretty girl even prettier." I know it was over the top. These were the kind of clothes most girls wear all the time, nothing fancy. Even knowing that, it felt good to hear the compliments. Screw feminism. I wanted to hear someone say I looked pretty.

I already felt that I had a stronger bond with Doug than I ever had with Connor. With Connor, I held back a part of myself. I certainly couldn't tell him I was promised to marry another guy. And I was afraid to tell him about my parents' strict beliefs. Either thing might scare him off. And I guess it eventually did. But Doug knew everything. I could be open with him. Our hotel room that night in Tulsa had only a king-size bed and no sofa. I won't go into details, but I gave myself to Doug that night. The wine helped, but I didn't regret it. At least not for a few days.

Houston

We slept late and got a leisurely start on our journey from Tulsa to Houston. After so many hours with Doug, I ran out of things to talk about and fell asleep several times on the drive. We got to Houston late. The house was a small three-bedroom, one-story brick structure in a neighborhood of similar homes. I noticed half the houses had burglar bars over the windows, including Doug's. It was a step down from my home back in St. Louis. Money must be tight, and I appreciated his willingness to help a girl in need.

Doug had housemates, but they were out and not expected back for hours so we had the house to ourselves. Doug said he would introduce me to his housemates and other friends tomorrow. The girls lived together in a larger house, which he said was like a sorority house. He said I could move into that house in a few days, but in the meantime, I would be with him. That was fine with me.

I met the housemates late in the morning. Doug was still in bed, but I wanted to see the place in the daylight, so I changed into a T-shirt and shorts and went out to the living room. I was looking out the window when one of the housemates came out of his bedroom wearing shorts and a faded red muscle shirt that said "Babe Patrol" in white lettering. He had a Chinese character tattooed on his right upper arm and tattoos of daggers, swords, and axes on each forearm.

When he saw me, he seemed overly enthusiastic. "Hey! I'm Blade. We've been so excited for you to join us!" When he finally reached me, he hugged me. Not a quick hug. More like the kind of hug you give a friend you haven't seen in a while. His greeting ended with, "If you need anything, let me know. But right now, I've got to take care of some business." He went to the bathroom. I found out later that the Chinese tattoo can mean a knife, sword, or blade.

The other housemate had a girlfriend over. He and his girlfriend both emerged from his bedroom wearing only their underwear. Just the bottoms. Although it was nearly lunchtime, the girl went to the kitchen and prepared cold breakfast cereal. The guy made himself a sandwich. They only acknowledged me after the girl sat down at the dining table.

She greeted me with, "Hey. You must be the new girl Bulldog brought in. I'm Reyna."

I know we're both girls, but I had a difficult time trying to not look at her chest. I'd never seen any girl's naked chest but my own. I tried hard to focus on her face as she spoke. Dark brown, almost black hair, brown eyes, and a slightly darker complexion than mine. I assumed she had some Native American blood in her. I wasn't sure how to react to an almost naked woman other than to say, "I'm Alia. I'm here with Doug."

The guy smiled as he looked me up and down. It didn't look like a friendly smile. It looked like a creepy smile. Or maybe it was my own projection. He could just be socially awkward. His lack of clothing didn't bother me as much. He was wearing boxers, which were as much as guys wear at the beach or the pool or even when playing basketball in the driveway.

"She's gonna give you some competition," the guy said to Reyna.

"You ready to trade me in, Shorty? You think I'm not good enough for you?" Reyna responded with a snort.

"You were good enough last night," Shorty answered with a grin.

"If you think you can do better, go ahead," Reyna said. "Maybe my nights off would be better without having to keep you happy."

"And what would you do with all your free time without me?"

"Maybe I'd watch TV. Or play video games. Or read a book."

"Ha. I've never seen you open a book," Shorty responded.

"Maybe I'll start today." She looked at me and added, "You can have him."

I didn't know if I was witnessing a lovers' quarrel or if they were just joking around. The whole conversation was awkward. But I was certain that I didn't want Shorty. Reyna could keep him. I just smiled politely and retreated to Doug's bedroom.

* * *

Doug walked me to the girls' house for lunch. In the daylight, I could see the neighborhood was showing its age. Fading paint, cracks in the driveways, and patches on some of the roofs. Doug explained that many of the houses were rentals.

The girls' house was a four-bedroom with a slightly bigger family room than the guys' house. It also had a large bedroom in the front that looked like it was once a formal living room. Instead of a closet, the room had two large cabinets that could hold hanging clothes. The bedrooms each had two twin mattresses on the floor. Cardboard boxes held the girls' belongings, the kind with removable lids. Some boxes were stacked by the beds to form makeshift nightstands, and some were in the closet. Each room had a long folding table with two mirrors, two baskets of makeup, and two stools.

I met several of the girls. The oldest was Lauren. She said she was Doug's sister.

"That's not how I would describe it," Doug said.

"Okay. How about stepsister?" She kissed him on the mouth. They have an unusual relationship that I'll explain later. In just three days, I'd been forming a rather close bond with Doug. So, I was a little surprised at their kiss and maybe a little uncertain about our bond.

I learned that Lauren got the master bedroom to herself. She was the house mom. Her room was the only bedroom that had a desk. It had its own bathroom, but the other girls were free to use it whenever they needed. With that many girls in the house, they needed to keep both bathrooms available.

Lunch was simple. It was fried chicken from KFC and salad that a couple of girls prepared. Everyone was friendly. When I asked what it was like to live with nine people in the house, they described it as a college dorm or sorority house, but I don't think any of them ever went to college. It didn't sound like they even graduated from high school. I wasn't sure they were even old enough to graduate from high school. One of the girls said they had their share of drama at the house, but they generally got along. And they reminded me that they only had eight girls in the house at the moment. One left to live with her boyfriend and work at a club. They joked as if she had grown up and graduated. They were holding the vacant bed for me while they decided whether to rearrange roommates.

After lunch, Lauren proposed a photo shoot. I had forgotten that Doug mentioned helping with a modeling business. I didn't think I was model material and said so. Lauren told me I have a nice shape and a pretty face. I was flattered to get such a compliment from a woman. She also said it never hurt to have photos ready in case someone might be interested.

She had me stand in front of a green screen in her bedroom and took a few photos, having me tilt my head this way and that. Doug sat on her bed, leaning against the headboard, and looking through his phone. She said my clothes were okay, but we need something dressier. One of the girls walked by wearing a red body-hugging minidress. Lauren called her in and noted that the girl and I were of similar size and told her to let me borrow the dress for the photos. The girl – Kelly – stripped off the dress right there on the spot and handed it to me. She stood in her black lace bra and panties like she was waiting for me to change in front of everyone.

At my hesitation, Lauren just told me to go ahead and change. I looked towards the bathroom, thinking to change in private. But Kelly's boldness shamed me for my lack of it.

Then Lauren told me, "Don't be shy, we're all girls here."

I guess Doug didn't count. He had already seen me without clothes, but Lauren and Kelly were practically strangers to me.

As I started stripping down, Kelly turned her attention to Doug. She noticed he was still wearing his shoes while on Lauren's bed.

I heard her mutter, "Beast," as she pulled his shoes off and tossed them onto the floor. Then she climbed over him to sit on the bed against the headboard next to him.

He put his arm around her shoulders and said, "Thanks for civilizing me, Beauty."

Lauren noticed me watching Kelly and Doug. Maybe she knew what I was thinking because she told me Kelly and Doug weren't a thing. She said they – meaning the girls and the guys I'd met that day – were all friendly with each other. And they seemed to have a rather casual attitude about clothes. I thought maybe that was the nature of the modeling industry.

That night we all went out to dinner and afterward played laser tag. Then we followed it up with smoking weed in the backyard of the girls' house. It was my first time. I think I giggled a lot as I walked back with the guys to their house that night.

The next night – Tuesday night – Doug and Blade would be driving the girls to a hotel for work. All three guys had crew cab pickups. I learned that the Dodge Challenger we drove from Missouri was a rental. Driving the girls was part of their daily routine. While Doug was away, Lauren took his place as a driver. That second night, Doug gave me the option of staying at his house by myself or going with them to work. I chose to go with them. But Shorty didn't join them.

"He's taking me out tonight," Laney told me at lunch. "It's my wifey night and I'm making him take me ice skating at the Galleria." She seemed excited. Does every city have a shopping mall called the Galleria? And is 'wifey night' Texas slang for a date?

I wondered if she knew that he was with Reyna Sunday night. I wasn't going to be the one to break the news. Besides, I didn't know which was the girlfriend and which was the side chick.

The Truth Comes Out

When Doug said they were going to a hotel for work, I imagined a hotel conference room or ballroom, set up with bright lights, photographers, and designer clothes. I had no idea how modeling worked. When we arrived, I saw it wasn't what I would call a hotel. It was a motel with room doors facing the parking lot. No conference room or ballroom. That's when I realized what was going on. The girls were prostitutes, and the guys were their pimps.

They called themselves managers. "Pimps have gold teeth and drive purple lowriders," Shorty explained when I used that term. "*We* manage a business."

Lauren and the guys got messages on their phones from clients and then directed them to a room where one of the girls was waiting. Sometimes the guys met the clients outside the motel rooms if the clients paid cash, periodically they walked back and forth in front of the rooms as if they were patrolling the place, and sometimes they just sat in their trucks, managing the assignments. I stayed with Doug in his truck.

I started feeling nauseous. I looked at Doug in a whole new light. "Is this what you want me to do? You brought me from St. Louis to be one of your hookers?" I felt like throwing up.

"I brought you here because you were in a bad situation and needed help," Doug said. "Me and my friends are trying to make the best out of bad circumstances. Most of the girls are runaways like you and can't get a job that pays enough to live on. Shelters aren't permanent places to live. And if they go to the cops, CPS will get involved and most likely send them back to the bad situation they ran away from."

He waved his hand towards the motel, towards the closed doors where the girls were. "All of them were messed up before we found them. All of them were abused. Some by family members. Some were working the streets. Some didn't even do it for money; they just did it for food and a place to stay. Men were exploiting them, and they had little control over it."

He reached across the center console and took my hand

"Isn't this just exploiting them more?" I asked as I pulled my hand away.

"This is way better than what they had before. This adds safety, control, and structure."

He made it sound so noble. I suspect he had given that speech before. But my nausea remained. The lessor of two evils is still evil. My father was abusive, but not sexually. I had no desire to join their team of "models".

My mind went back to the events of the day. The girls didn't act afraid of the guys. Lauren and Kelly seemed extra friendly with Doug. Delaney, known as Laney around the house, seemed to look forward to her date with Shorty. And Reyna was with Shorty a couple of nights ago, joking around with him. So maybe Doug was right about their current situation being better than what they experienced before. Or maybe their behavior was a coping mechanism.

I told Doug I wasn't doing that. He told me to keep an open mind, and that everyone must do things they don't like at some point. I thought of my sister's marriage. She didn't want it but wasn't strong enough to stop it.

I didn't realize how late the group stayed at the motel. I eventually fell asleep in the truck.

I stayed with Doug again that night. It was the fifth night with him, but the first time I felt uncomfortable, knowing what he and his group were doing. But he has this way about him. He could distract me from my concerns and move the conversation to something safe. Is charming the right word? He was charming and smooth. I was assigned to his room for now. The girls said they were still not ready for me at their house as they were still working out room arrangements. Where else would I go?

In the first two days, Shorty and Blade also got into loud arguments three times with name-calling that involved each other's mother. But later they seemed to be best buddies. They joked about hooking up with me. I wasn't sure if they were serious, but knowing the business they were in, the comments scared me. Doug reassured me they were good guys and the girls trusted them.

Starting my Second Life

Wednesday, Doug took me out to see the city. At lunch, he ordered a margarita and teased me about my inability to order alcohol while he could. It's cliché that when faced with a bad situation, people often drown their troubles with alcohol. After the revelation of the night before, I kind of felt jealous that I couldn't order a drink and I even said so. On the way home, Doug stopped and bought tequila. Then he drove us to a park to drink it out of paper cups with pictures of balloons printed on them. He said it was a delayed celebration of a new life in Houston.

When we got back to the house, he led me into our – his – bedroom, closed the door, and made it clear that he wanted to play. I liked Doug a lot. My Prince Eric. But I was a little hesitant about his friends being in the next room and I told him that. However, he has this way of making everything seem alright. We were standing next to the bed, and I was in the middle of undressing and had my shirt off when Shorty and Blade came in.

I yelled "Hey!" and I thought Doug would yell at them to get out. Instead, he put his hand over my mouth.

He said, "It's okay. We're all family here," as if that made what was about to happen okay. Then he pushed me so hard that I fell backward onto the bed. Blade went to the opposite side of the bed and grabbed my wrists and pulled my arms up over my head until I was stretched out sideways across the bed. He forced my wrists down against the mattress, like a position of surrender. Shorty leaned down and pressed his forearms onto my thighs, holding my lower body against the bed.

At first, I wasn't sure if this was a terrible prank. But when Shorty slid his forearms up my thighs, keeping his weight on them, I realized it was something else. When he began stroking my bare skin at the waistline of my jeans, I screamed, "No!"

Bulldog leaned over and put his hand over my mouth to stifle my screams. I struggled to sit up, to roll over, to do anything. But the weight of the men – the friends – on my arms and legs kept me pinned to the bed.

"I'm going to the store," Bulldog announced. "I'll be back in about an hour." He put his face close to mine and removed his hand.

"No!" I shouted again, terrified. I couldn't believe he was leaving me like that.

He kissed me and said, "Be nice to these guys. I'll bring back dinner. You like fajitas, right?"

I closed my eyes tightly and all I could think of was "No." And it wasn't about the fajitas. I'm not even sure if the word came out of my mouth or just stayed in my head. Just, "No."

Then Shorty unfastened my jeans. "Just relax, Sweetie. Relax and enjoy it."

No!

It was not a prank.

* * *

When the guys were finished, they left the room and started talking about football as if everything was normal. I got up and peeked through the door and into the living room. The guys were sitting on the sofa, already drinking beer. Blade saw me and lifted his bottle in acknowledgment.

"Beer?" he asked.

I yelled – not words, just a wail – and slammed the bedroom door. I hurried to the window, pulled back the curtains, and reached for the window latch before realizing the burglar bars on the other side would prevent an escape. I didn't see anyone outside to call for help. I let loose another wail in anger, frustration, and – I don't know what to call it – raw emotion. I was in a prison.

I went back to the bed, stumbling over something on the floor. My clothes. I had been walking around naked except for my bra. I'm so stupid! Don't trust people you meet online. Don't get in cars with strangers. Stupid. Stupid. Stupid. Was this my new life? To be passed around from man to man? To screw strangers at a cheap motel? It was punishment for making stupid choices and for defying my father. I crawled under the covers, pulled them up over my head, curled up, and cried.

Bulldog and Lauren came back with food, and I could hear Shorty tell them that I was a little upset. A little? I was in the fetal position and the pillow was already soaked with tears and drool.

Bulldog came into the bedroom to announce dinner was ready. He even pulled back the sheet to kiss me. My betrayer. I couldn't believe he could act like nothing happened. I turned away and pulled the sheet back over my head.

He said, "Look, Blade and Shorty are good guys. Just think of them as an extension of me. We share everything and we look after each other, just as we look after the girls."

Lauren came in and kicked Doug out of the room. She sat on the bed and rubbed my back. She said, "I know this is a big adjustment for you, but you're gonna be okay. We'll make sure of it."

Then she said, "Look," as she pulled the sheet back from my head. "They left something for you." She held up a wad of money. "Your first earnings!"

I had paused my crying to look, but now I just cried harder. They paid me for their time with me.

"I'm not a prostitute!" I yelled.

She ignored that and continued the money talk. "Normally, I would keep it for you to pay for food, housing, and all that. We ain't a charity. But since this is your first time, we'll let you keep it all. Maybe you can use it to buy nicer clothes and makeup."

Eventually, I heard the guys leave to pick up the girls to take them to the hotel. Lauren stayed with me.

Earnings? I told Lauren I wasn't working to earn that money. I was raped. I told her what they did to me.

She told me I was lucky. Lucky? If she was trying to comfort me, it wasn't working. First "earnings", now "lucky". Was I lucky to be raped by two men who were supposed to be friends? Was I lucky to exchange money for sex? What the hell!

"You're sixteen, right?" she said.

I just nodded.

"And you weren't a virgin. So, you didn't lose your innocence today."

I wasn't sure where she was going with that. I asked, "How do you know that?"

She said, "From your DMs. You *banged* your boyfriend from school and later when your father found out, he beat you for it."

Her actual language was cruder than that. I won't use the actual language she and the others used in their normal conversations. It included a lot of words that don't meet school guidelines.

I was surprised Doug would share such details of our conversation. "Doug showed you our DMs?"

"Sweet Pea, Kelly showed me your messages. She was the one messaging you on Bulldog's account."

Kelly had catfished me using Doug's name and photos. Of course, she showed Doug so he would know the details of my life. And he did his own DMs on the day he met me. But the rest was Kelly.

"Why did she use Doug's account instead of her own?"

"She did DM under her own account too, but you seemed to connect better with Doug. Plus, Doug had a longer Instagram history than Kelly."

I guess after getting dumped by Connor, I took comfort in believing another guy was interested in my miserable life. One of my many foolish mistakes.

She continued, "So, basically, tonight you experienced something that you had done several times before on your own.

And you didn't lose anything from it. You got something." She tapped the wad of money sitting on the nightstand.

Then she told me, "I was eleven when I lost my virginity, and I didn't get to choose who with. Maybe you don't think so now, but the guys in this house don't want to hurt you. They'll take care of you. That's why you're lucky."

Maybe she thought her talk was helping, but she just made me confused. I didn't know how to respond to her story about being eleven for her first. But I still didn't feel lucky.

Lauren told me to toughen up and couldn't believe I hadn't taken a shower. She said that's what they all do after a night with their customers. Clean up. Get dressed.

When I didn't move, she yanked the sheet back. When I still didn't move, she slapped my butt. Hard. Like my father did when I talked back or questioned his authority. When my father did it, I would try my hardest not to cry. But since I'd already been crying, this time I couldn't hold it back. I let out a yell and cried louder.

Through the tears, I managed to get up and go to the bathroom to shower. Only then did I notice the bruises on my wrists where Blade had grabbed them to hold me down. Lauren followed me into the bathroom. I think she was concerned I might try to do something. The bathroom didn't have a window to escape through, so maybe she thought I would try to hurt myself. Anyway, she sat on the toilet while I showered.

Despite my helplessness, some of my rebellious streak came out. That's why I kept getting in trouble with my father. Here in this prison-house, I turned to face Lauren through the frosted glass shower door. I couldn't see the details of her face, only a blurry form that I knew was her. "How can you act like this is normal?" I yelled. "What's wrong with you people?!"

My father would have beaten me for talking to him like that, although he would wait until I came out of the bathroom. Fortunately, Lauren was not my father.

Lauren

"Allie, this is better than what we had before," Lauren told me. That's also what Bulldog had said. Was it true or did they rehearse their story together?

She called me Allie. Not short for Alia, but short for Alicia. That was my new name around clients, but just Allie around the house. I don't think the other girls even know my real name. Then she told me how she got started.

"When I was eleven years old, my mother had a baby with her boyfriend, Ronnie. He lived with us. The baby slept in their bedroom. That's when Ronnie started his nighttime visits to my bedroom. And he wasn't there to chat, if you know what I mean. He threatened to kill me and my mom if I ever told anyone about it.

"Doug was Ronnie's son. He started coming to visit every other weekend when I was twelve and he was nine, with longer visits in the summer. He slept on the sofa in the living room since our trailer house had only two bedrooms, one for mom, Ronnie, and the baby, and the other for me. The house wasn't in a trailer park, but the neighborhood was only about one step above one. I still call myself trailer park trash. The neighborhood was a mix of trailer houses, ancient wood-frame houses, and small commercial businesses.

"One night Ronnie visited my room on a weekend when Doug was over. The sounds of my protests, soft as they were so as not to alert my mother, were enough to wake up Doug. He came to my room to see what was going on. Even at nine years old, he knew his father shouldn't be on me with his pants down. He yelled for his daddy to get off me and he began pounding on Ronnie's back.

"Ronnie twisted around and grabbed Doug's arm. That was good for me, because Ronnie got off me, but bad for Doug. Ronnie put his hand over Doug's mouth and told him that if he woke up my mother or told my mother about his "special times" with me, he would kill me and my mother. Then he shoved Doug out of the room, locked the door, and finished what he came for. I don't know how many times he'd already done this. I cried less and less after each time."

Then why did Lauren think it was fine for me? Was it because I wasn't a child when the guys attacked me? That I could handle it better?

"After Ronnie left, Doug came back in and climbed into my bed, and wrapped his arms around me. He told me his daddy shouldn't do that and he was mad and sad at the same time. I hugged him back. That's what started our special bond. After that night, Doug slept with me whenever he came over. We were both skinny enough to share the twin bed without either of us falling off. I think Doug thought that with him in my room, his dad wouldn't come anymore. It was sweet that a little nine-year-old tried to protect me. The new sleeping arrangement may have helped a little because Ronnie didn't come as often when Doug was over, but it didn't stop him completely. When he was in the mood, he would just drag Doug out and lock the door.

"After a couple of years, mom made me share my room with little Dalton. Ronnie didn't visit as often after that but didn't stop, either. When I was fifteen, I got tired of sharing a room with a toddler and complained over and over. Mom arranged for me to live with my aunt a few streets over. Doug would still come to see me when it was his weekend to visit his dad. Sometimes he even spent the night. It was a bigger bed. My aunt thought it was strange that we would sleep in the same bed, but he was just a kid, so it wasn't a big deal."

As Lauren told her story, I started to think that Doug got an early start in trying to rescue girls in trouble. Then I had to catch myself with that thought. Doug didn't really rescue me. He captured me. Lauren continued her story.

"When I was seventeen, my aunt moved away, so I had to move back in with my mother and Ronnie. She was calling him her husband by then, but they'd never officially gotten married. One Saturday my mom was at her waitressing gig and Ronnie decided he didn't need to wait until nighttime. He'd had a few too many beers at lunch and thought early afternoon would be a good time to visit my bedroom. I was old enough now to put up a fight, but Ronnie was bigger and stronger than me.

"Ronnie forgot it was Doug's weekend. I guess Doug heard enough before he came in that he knew what was going on. He came in with a baseball bat and hit Ronnie in the head with it. Twice. Ronnie fell to the floor and moaned. I grabbed the bat from Doug and hit Ronnie another couple of times until he was silent and still. He looked dead. I told Doug we need to leave and hide out. I didn't feel guilty for killing Ronnie, but I didn't want to go to jail either.

"I grabbed my backpack and a duffle bag and stuffed them with everything I could fit into them. I also got all my mom's cash from the dresser drawer where she thought she was hiding it. Doug took all the cash from Ronnie's wallet, then put the wallet back in Ronnie's pocket. We ran away. I was seventeen and Doug was fourteen.

"We took a bus to Houston and eventually found ourselves living in an ancient, abandoned RV in the vacant lot next to a rundown house in a rundown neighborhood. At least we thought it was abandoned. Its tires were flat, and weeds were growing around it. I doubt the engine would start. The inside smelled like cigarettes and dirty gym socks. The good thing was that it was hooked up to water and electricity like someone once lived there full-time. This pimply-faced teen from the rundown house saw us go in one day and said it belonged to his family and they already had to run off other homeless people trying to live there. And he said when he told his dad about us, his dad would run us off, too.

"We later found out he had no dad. It was just him and his overworked mom. The RV had belonged to his grandfather who had moved to a nursing home."

I wondered if I could find a place like that to get away from Lauren and her prostitute gang.

Lauren continued, "I told him we could pay him to not tell and to let us live there. We would be more careful not to let people see us coming and going. When he asked if we had money, I got worried. If I told him we did, he might try to steal it and then kick us out. I told him no. Then he asked how we could pay him. That's when I made my deal with the devil.

"I would be his girlfriend if he let us stay there. He agreed. Doug wasn't happy about the arrangement.

"Then our teenage landlord brought friends over. I was being pimped by a high school kid. I convinced them that the least they could do was give us food and stuff to live on. Then the boys' older brothers started coming around. Then the uncles. We'd lost control of the situation and I felt just as hopeless as I had with Ronnie.

"I started calling Doug Bulldog in front of those guys. I needed him to look and sound tough, so the boys didn't get too pushy. They had a hard time believing that some of the things they saw in pornos didn't work in real life. There are limits to what a body can do. I needed Doug to tell them that no meant no for certain things they wanted."

Nevermind. I was no longer envious of the RV.

"Doug hated the arrangement and wanted us to find somewhere else to live. But we'd looked before and there weren't any good options for runaways with little cash. Doug was doing odd jobs, sometimes waiting for jobs with the day laborers in the parking lot of the hardware store. But the money wasn't enough for two to live on. And who would rent an apartment to a couple of kids?

"The work made Doug look tougher. When he pretended to be an illegal immigrant people wouldn't ask many questions. I guess having a Mexican mother and speaking Spanish with her helped him fit in. The other immigrants viewed him as a gringo, but he could fool the employers. His work meant that he wasn't always with me when the men would come around to the RV, which was sometimes kind of scary for me.

"Around Christmas, I checked my mother's Facebook account on a library computer. I hadn't done that since we left. Ronnie wasn't dead. He'd been in the hospital, but eventually recovered and was smiling in photos with my mom and Dalton. What a happy little family. In one of the captions, my mom called Dalton her little Sweet Pea. That's what Mom used to call me before Dalton was born. Her Sweet Pea.

"I called her from a phone in the library. Ronnie had told her that he caught me and Doug having sex and when he tried to stop us, we attacked him. When I told her the truth, she called me a liar. She said I should be thankful Ronnie didn't press charges. That was it. I haven't spoken to her since then.

"I told Doug he should go back to his mother and live a normal life, but he wouldn't leave me. I'm glad he didn't. He's a good guy."

The hell he is! Good guys don't help their friends rape a girl!

Initiation

Lauren was quiet for a moment before continuing. "Bulldog and I realized we needed to change the dynamic. One thing led to another and here we are. It still involves *screwing* men we don't know, but we're in control."

By "we" I assume she was referring to the other girls, not Bulldog.

That's how I learned what was wrong with those people. They were so messed up that sex with strangers in a "controlled environment" was better than what they had before.

She told me she had already sacrificed her time with Bulldog for me. And she warned me that when he returned from the motel, I'd better treat him with respect, because he was sacrificing his time with me, too.

After my shower, Lauren grabbed Bulldog's bottle of tequila, walked me to the girls' house, and made me eat dinner with her. After a couple of beers and a shot of tequila, she insisted on painting my nails. She even did my toes. Either the alcohol didn't affect her, or she didn't have as much as I had, because the nail job was pretty good.

I went through a range of emotions. Terror, betrayal, disgust. At one point I hated all of them. Then pity. I even teetered on the edge of understanding after Lauren's story. Then I was angry again. Knowing how bad it was, how could she – they – drag me into this? And now she was holding my hand and gently painting my nails like we were girlfriends. The whole evening was very confusing.

I was stuck, and Doug and Lauren knew it. I couldn't go back home. My father would either refuse to take me back, or he would first beat the crap out of me and then refuse to take me back. Or worse. In my father's traditional culture overseas, daughters were sometimes killed for lesser offenses.

Bulldog and his group didn't come to my rescue because I had such a miserable story. They got me partly because I was pretty enough that men would want me, miserable enough to want to run away, and naïve enough to believe strangers' charitable motives. If I went to the authorities, they would send me back home to my doom. I was a mark they could exploit.

After smoking a joint with Lauren on the back patio, I fell asleep in her bed.

* * *

Bulldog wasn't Prince Eric; he was Ursula. He tricked me with his charm and fake kindness, teasing me with the hope of a better life, all the while forcing me into a different kind of captivity. I couldn't call Doug by his real name anymore; it sounded too normal. He was a dog. I started calling him what his friends called him: Bulldog. If I had thought about it at the time, I might have started calling his friends Jetsam and Flotsam.

Or maybe Lauren was Ursula and Doug was just another minion.

Blade and Shorty did not seem to me to be the good guys that Lauren and Bulldog made them out to be. Besides raping unsuspecting girls, I saw them get into shoving matches with each other over little things. Blade carried a knife that he kept in a sheath attached to his belt. He liked to pull it out and twirl it around or throw it at a dartboard hanging on the wall in the living room. There were a lot of holes in the wall around that dart board.

One of the girls had bruises on her arm and cheek. I found out they were from Blade. According to Lauren, the girl was with Blade the night before and he got a little too rough with her in bed, so she crapped on his bed. He got mad at that and shoved her, knocking her onto the floor. The other girls laughed at that.

* * *

The day after my rape and girl time with Lauren – it sounds so casual, doesn't it? – I woke up next to Bulldog, still in Lauren's bed. I don't know where Lauren slept. She was at the computer when I woke up.

After lunch or breakfast or whatever meal it was, Reyna walked me back to the guys' house, but Bulldog stayed back. Reyna told him that Lauren missed him. Over the weeks, I noticed Lauren and Bulldog would often drive away together in the early afternoons. Sometimes they came back with supplies and sometimes not.

At the guys' house, Reyna went to the refrigerator and got four beers. One each for herself, Shorty, Blade, and me. I didn't ask for one, she just gave it to me. I started to go hide in my bedroom – Bulldog's bedroom – with my beer but Reyna grabbed my arm and pulled me to sit next to her on the sofa. Blade and Shorty sat at the kitchen table.

She said, "If we're all gonna live together, we have to be able to have a conversation."

I didn't feel much like making small talk, but she tried. She asked about the difference between the weather in St. Louis versus Houston. She asked if I liked to watch any shows on TV, and she told me her own TV show preferences. Occasionally, Blade or Shorty would add to the conversation. Reyna also told me that she and Shorty had been together for a long time, and they were working the streets before meeting Lauren and Bulldog. Lauren proposed they team up to look out for each other. It sounded good, but at the time, she was still uncertain of the deal.

"It just sounded like Lauren wanted to be my pimp," she said. "Something I'd tried to avoid."

I asked, "Isn't that what Shorty is?"

"Shorty didn't set a quota or hold me captive. I decided on my schedule. And I could turn down men I didn't like. Shorty was there to make sure the guys paid and behaved."

"Like a pimp."

Reyna ignored the comment. "It's hard to trust people in this business, so I just blew Lauren off. But then Lauren sent Bulldog to me as a paying customer. I didn't recognize him at first. But while we were doing it, he didn't act like a customer. He was more concerned with pleasing me, than having me please him. He sweet-talked me into meeting with them to go over a business plan. Bulldog has this way about him."

"But I'm still your number one, right?" Shorty interrupted.

Reyna answered, "Sure, Shorty. You're my number one." I thought I detected a hint of sarcasm in her voice.

Blade laughed and punched Shorty in the arm.

Yes, I agreed with Reyna's assessment of Bulldog. He had a way about him. I couldn't explain why, but I began to relax. My rapists were in the same room and yet I was having a normal conversation with the girlfriend of one of them. Well, the topic wasn't normal, but the atmosphere seemed normal.

Shorty came to the sofa and sat next to Reyna. "Reyna didn't tell you that some of the gang pimps were starting to harass her, trying to get her to join them. At one point, one of them tried to drag her to a car. I didn't usually hang around while she worked. She would text if she needed me. We had an arrangement but seeing her with the men was a little… uh… weird for me, so I usually hung out in the park or something. But that night I was in the area and saw the guy try to drag her to his car. I drove up and bumped my car into his to get his attention. Then I got out and explained that taking Reyna was a bad idea."

"Shorty showed him his gun," Reyna explained. "He can be persuasive in a different way than Bulldog." Reyna reached over and patted Shorty's leg. "Just a few more minutes," she said to him before leaning over to kiss him.

Reyna knew what happened between me and the guys, but it didn't seem to bother her. They view things a lot differently than most people. Multiple sex partners were just part of the business. And if one forced himself on the new girl, it was just an unpleasant experience. Unpleasant for the new girl, not for the guys. Rape had no meaning to them.

"Why are you giving him all the attention, Reyna?" Blade said. "Save some lovin' for me."

"Are you feeling left out?" she said as she stood up. She walked over to Blade and asked, "You think you've got enough for both of us?"

Shorty scooted over next to me on the sofa. I should have been alarmed but, strangely, I wasn't. I felt relaxed. Reyna and Blade disappeared into Blade's bedroom.

Shorty was first. Blade finished up. I knew what was happening and I protested, but I didn't have the will to resist. I learned later that Reyna had spiked my beer. The guys each left money on the coffee table when they were done, as if that made it better. For me, it was a reminder of my hopelessness. Reyna gathered up my clothes from the living room floor and walked me to the shower.

* * *

Afterward, I laid down on the bed and pulled the covers up over my head again and passed out. When I woke up, I heard Doug and Lauren in the living room, and I peeked out. Lauren saw me and smiled. She dared to ask me if today was better than yesterday. I started to complain to her, but she cut me off and told me to get over it.

Doug told me he could arrange for me to go back to my parents if that's what I wanted. He was the good cop to Lauren's bad cop.

Lauren said, "Fine, but you may want to see this first." She handed me her phone with the screen open to a recent news article about a father in Ohio who killed his daughter for dishonoring the family when she was caught having sex with her infidel boyfriend. I felt sick to my stomach. When it came to religious fundamentalism, my father was close to the extreme.

The money from Blade and Shorty was still on the coffee table. Lauren took it, saying it was for room and board. I think she just gave it back to the guys.

A Proud Moment

The night after that, they took me to the motel to meet clients, saying they were giving me a lighter schedule than the other girls to ease me into the business. I didn't get a spiked drink that night because, they said, clients prefer girls who are alert, not passed out.

When the second customer left, I ran into the bathroom and leaned over the toilet just in time to barf into the bowl. When there was nothing left to give, I curled up on the floor of the bathroom and cried.

Bulldog came into the room and called out cheerfully, "Allie, how's my girl?"

"I can't do this," I told him when I could stop sobbing long enough to talk. "I just can't."

He sat down on the edge of the bathtub and rubbed my back. "Yes, you can."

"No, I can't."

"I know it's hard at first, but you can." He slid off the tub and down onto the floor next to me. He put his arm under me and lifted me into a sitting position.

"One summer when Lauren and I were on our own, I worked for a company that cleaned septic tanks. The truck didn't have A/C. The temperature was in the upper nineties, and I would sweat buckets. The job was literally cleaning up other people's *crap*. It stank. I stank. When I got home in the evening, I could barely make it to the shower. I'd fall asleep on the sofa before dinner. It sucked. But each day, I got a little more used to it and it got a little more tolerable. We needed the money."

"I would rather do that," I said.

He put his arm around my shoulders. "I'm just saying, you can get used to a job you don't like. It pays your food, rent, clothes, and stuff." He paused before adding, "And you get air conditioning." He smiled at his lame joke.

I didn't think it was funny. I felt like crying more, but nothing came out. Eventually, I just said again, "I can't."

"Only a few more tonight. We're easing you into a full schedule." He pulled me up to a standing position, wrapped his arms around me, and kissed me.

He was trying to act like a boyfriend who cared about me. But someone who cared wouldn't turn me into a whore.

"My brave girl is strong. You can do this. Now let's get ready for the next customer. I'll straighten up your bed while you get yourself cleaned up."

I learned later that if Bulldog couldn't help the girls overcome their initial reluctance through encouragement, Blade and Shorty would help them overcome it with a cattle prod. More force than that might result in a girl missing a day of work and she would have to make up her quota of customers over the next few days. I saw the cattle prod, but it would be a long time before I saw them use it on us. One time at the guys' house,

Blade shocked Shorty with it and Shorty took a swing at him, then chased him around the yard. I thought it was just a prop to keep us reluctant girls in line.

My brain shut down in the middle of the fourth customer. I assume I finished the evening's business, but I have no memory of the last two clients at all. However, I do remember that Lauren and Bulldog came in after everything was over.

She hugged me and said, "Sweet Pea, you did great tonight! I know it was hard for you, but you pulled yourself together and did it."

"I knew you could do it," Bulldog said.

Lauren finished by saying, "I'm proud of you."

I replied, "Thank you."

How stupid am I? They're proud of me for having sex with strangers that they pushed on me, and I was thanking them. Afterward, all the girls came around and gave me hugs. Most congratulated me for getting through the first day. Only one – Sarah – said "sorry." I don't know how to explain what was going on in my head. I felt disgusted for what I'd just done and relieved that I'd gotten through it. But I actually appreciated their praise. Yes, I'm stupid.

We girls all showered at the motel before going home because there weren't enough bathrooms at the girls' house. Not that it mattered to me; I was still in Bulldog's room at the guy's house, and it had its own bathroom. Yet I just wanted to shower as soon as possible to try to wash the filth from my brain. Lauren held my hand on the ride home and that night I stayed with

Bulldog again. He stroked my hair and gave me more compliments but didn't try to get more intimate than that.

The next night, they put a roofie in my beer before work. Enough to help me relax, but not to knock me out. I remembered all the clients that night. How many other jobs not only encourage workers to drink before starting work but also hand out the booze?

There was no chance of going back home now. If my father found out what I did, I'm pretty sure a tugboat would find my body floating face down in the Mississippi.

Eventually, working nights had me checking the clock after every client, counting down the time until the night was over, and mentally celebrating the halfway mark and the three-quarter mark. Then the sigh of relief that it was over. At least over for that night.

Then Tylenol and more alcohol. I know you're not supposed to combine alcohol with drugs but at that time I didn't care. I just wanted to reduce the constant soreness.

The physical aspect was only part of the exhaustion each night, but the mental aspect may have contributed more to the exhaustion than the physical. Each night, as soon as I walked into that motel room, the wall around my mind started to form, to solidify. Lauren and the others made it clear that I had to fully participate with the clients. But that didn't mean my mind had to participate. It was how I kept the repulsion of the activity from driving me insane.

I once talked to Kanya about it. She assured me that my mental separation was normal and, as long as I could still function in bed, was acceptable.

"After all," Kanya said. "The man doesn't want *you*. He wants your body."

Reyna was a bit more descriptive of that concept. "We're just a warm, wet hole."

Keeping my mind separate from the physical took effort and by the end of each night, I was mentally exhausted. The Tylenol was for the physical and the alcohol for the mental. It helped me lower that wall and fall asleep.

* * *

I was sold fifteen times that first week, not counting the fake initiation sales to Blade and Shorty.

-Review Session One-

"Hi, Ms. Amanda," Alia said when the door opened. "Did you have a chance to review my paper?"

"Oh, Honey," Amanda muttered as she wrapped her arms around Alia. "I'm so sorry you went through that."

Alia almost dropped the folder in her hand as Amanda squeezed her tight. Hugs from Ms. Amanda were common, but they usually didn't come with sadness in her eyes or last as long as this one.

"Ms. Amanda, you're already treating me differently. That's why I don't like telling people about it."

"I'm sorry, Alia. I can see why you wouldn't want to think about this. There I was, telling you it would be good for you, but now I think I made a mistake."

"No, it's okay. You were right. I needed to write everything down. Eventually, I'll put it in a box on a high shelf in the closet and may never look at it again."

"Okay," Amanda acknowledged. "I'll try to contain myself. But I just want to give you another hug."

In mid-embrace, Alia said, "Ty started acting weird about it, too."

"You got Ty to read this? I'm surprised because Ty doesn't read anything."

"Yeah, I found that out. He said he wouldn't be good at spelling or grammar, but I wanted his opinion anyway on the overall writing. I figured he could at least do that."

"And that convinced him to read it?"

"No. He got me to read it to him."

"Oh my gosh. You're braver than me. I would not be able to read that out loud to anyone, let alone a guy friend."

"Yeah. I didn't think about that at first. I was fine until I got to the part where Shorty and Blade came into the bedroom. I think I must have turned red or something, 'cause Ty asked if I was alright. I couldn't read that out loud to Ty."

"What was his take on it?"

"He actually read the next part himself. He just said, 'Your paper's fine.' Then he went outside and slammed the door and started doing chin-ups on the tree in the back yard. In the dark."

"I hug. He does something physical," Amanda summarized. She motioned for Alia to have a seat on the sofa as she went to the kitchen.

"Can I get you something to drink? The hardest thing I have is Dr Pepper."

"That's okay. Do you have lemonade?"

"Lemonade it is. If I had whiskey, I'd have already had a few shots myself."

She returned to the living room with a glass of lemonade for Alia and a can of Dr Pepper for herself. Then she picked up Alia's paper from the end table and passed it to Alia.

"Nothing major. I marked a few spelling and grammar mistakes. I also made some notes in the margins where I thought there might be a better way to phrase a sentence."

Alia took the report and placed it in the folder she'd been carrying. Then she removed a fresh set of papers and held it out to Amanda.

"What's that?" Amanda asked.

"It's the next part."

"There's more? You're paper's already way past the five-page requirement. I didn't know you were writing more."

"I was there a year. The part I gave you last time only covered the first few days."

"Alia, I don't know how you kept your sanity. I would have melted into a puddle of emotions."

"I did. When they guys came into the bedroom and Bulldog left, I was more terrified than I'd ever been in my whole life."

She took a sip of lemonade, then opened the paper that Amanda had marked up. She flipped through the pages, noting Amanda's markings, but not stopping to read them. Upon reaching the end she put it back in the folder.

Her voice was lower, quieter, when she added, "I'm not sure which was more terrifying, getting attacked by Blade and Shorty, or that first night they put me in the motel room and told me to wait."

House rules

I knew the other girls had some freedom. They could walk out and disappear. At least that's what it looked like to me. Sometimes they came back with snacks from a convenience store. I was still in the guys' house, and someone was with me all the time, as if they feared I would sneak out and never return. Or maybe it was a suicide watch. I asked when they would stop babysitting me.

Shorty's response was, "When you can let loose a loud, smelly fart in front of us, the kind that rattles the windows, then we'll know you're one of us, family."

I didn't want to be one of them.

* * *

I later found out it was Lauren's idea to have Blade and Shorty rape me because I wasn't coming around to their way of life fast enough. She wanted me out there bringing in the cash.

My life hadn't been as bad as theirs. Sure, my father was abusive, but I often instigated it. I could have been submissive like my sister and avoided the worst of his angry punishments. The situation I was really trying to escape was a future in a loveless marriage to a stranger. And the possibility that the stranger might be just as abusive as my father. I didn't have an example of a good marriage.

The other girls seemed to accept their lives. They laughed with each other, and they argued with each other. They were friends with each other.

None of them had pity on me, except maybe Sarah. I should just shut up and do what everyone else was doing. Put in my time at the motels to earn the right to have a roof over my head and food on the table, and maybe even put a little money away for when I turned eighteen and could move out. Eighteen was when a person would be able to open a bank account and sign an apartment lease without a parent. It was when they could earn money in other ways that were available to high school dropouts, such as dancing at a strip club. That was what they looked forward to.

I learned to hold my tears to avoid their condemnation.

* * *

Our prostitution ring had rules. Some were official and some were just what I learned after a while. Most were dictated by Lauren.

One:

They would not do business with pedophiles. Lauren was pretty adamant about that. If a client asked for an underage girl, they sent him away or didn't respond to his message.

Two:

They would only take girls who could pass for eighteen. Clients are told all the girls are at least eighteen, regardless of their actual age. This is related to rule one, a way to avoid pedophiles.

The exception was Kanya, who was eighteen even though she looked like a kid, due to her short stature and Asian features. She came to them when she was much younger, but the other girls at the time helped her with makeup to make her look older. They often put her with their youngest clients who were closer to her age than the typical client. They also got her a noticeable tattoo on her left shoulder to help her look older. After all, kids don't have tattoos, right?

Three:

No one worked on Monday. It was our Monday Funday. Sometimes we did things as a group, like bowling or ice skating or the Kemah Boardwalk. Once we went on an overnight trip to Six Flags Fiesta Texas in San Antonio. Other times, we were on our own.

Four:

We had wifey nights, what you would call date nights in the outside world.

The girls referred to themselves as wifey when it came to dates with our own guys. As in, "I'm not working tonight, I'm Blade's wifey." Sometimes we girls referred to ourselves collectively as wifeys. As much as I disliked the whole operation,

I also used the term. I assumed the guys would be called "hubby". One time when I was getting ready for a date with Shorty, I referred to him as "hubby". The girls laughed at me. Apparently, the girls are wifeys, but the guys are not hubbies.

Each girl gets a wifey date night every week with one of the guys. It was a different day of the week for each girl and was either Sunday, Tuesday, Wednesday, or Thursday. It involved going out one-on-one like a real date and often started with dinner at a nice restaurant followed by something fun like go-carts or a movie. We rotated among the guys.

One week it would be a little wifey night and the next week it would be a big wifey night. Big wifey night always ended with sleeping over with the guy. And, yes, it almost always involved sex. On rare occasions, the date would be an overnight trip to somewhere like Galveston, San Antonio, or Lake Conroe. When we did those, we stayed at a nice hotel, not like the cheap motels where we worked. Those didn't happen very often.

Little wifey night was a shorter version of big wifey night. We had to help take the girls to the motel before we could start our date, and after the date, the guys would drop us off at the girls' house and then go to the motel to keep an eye on things and help bring the other girls back when they were done.

Lauren and Reyna implemented wifey nights after one of their early recruits confessed to feeling worthless and emotionally isolated by the dehumanizing nature of their work. She was envious of the relationships Lauren and Reyna had. Lauren had always had Bulldog, but Reyna still understood the girl's viewpoint since she had worked the streets for two years before Shorty came along. With input from the other working girls, Reyna and Lauren decided the best way to solve the issue was to share Bulldog and Shorty with the group. As you can imagine, the guys didn't object. The men's goal for wifey night was to make each girl feel valued and less likely to leave.

When the group was small, each wifey night was a big wifey night, but as they added members, they developed an alternating schedule of big dates and little dates.

Only one guy could do a big wifey night at a time because they always wanted two guys at the motel on weekdays and all three on Fridays and Saturdays. Some girls were disappointed if their night got pushed back for something. I must admit that after I was there a while, I looked forward to wifey nights.

Five:

The clients must always use condoms. Lauren made it clear that she didn't want us getting pregnant or catching STDs. She wasn't concerned about our health, though. It was about money. She didn't want us to miss work and spend money to deal with a pregnancy or the treatment of a disease.

Some of the girls occasionally let a guy go without protection if he secretly gave the girl a big tip in advance. It's risky.

Six:

They charged clients more if they asked for a specific girl. And Lauren would give that extra amount in cash to the requested girl for her to spend however she wanted. This was their incentive for us girls to treat the clients well enough to keep them coming back. Repeat clients were safer than first-timers. There was less risk of one being an undercover cop or a violent abuser.

Some girls used their bonus money to buy nicer clothes or a bicycle or a computer or things like that. Kanya was saving up for a car. Except they wouldn't let me buy a phone until I proved myself. I think they were afraid I would call the police or my parents or something.

Seven:

We girls had to get a tattoo on the back of our necks of a butterfly with a dollar sign for the body.

The tattoo was Reyna's idea. She came up with the *dollarfly* design. The tattoo was a sign to any gang pimps that we already belonged to a stable. Although the gang pimps generally didn't come around the motels where we DollarFly girls worked, we were instructed to casually lift our hair and show the tattoo if any unexpected man approached.

Tattoo shops aren't supposed to tattoo minors without a parent's permission, but they found a tattoo artist who was willing to ignore the rules. According to one of the girls, Lauren offered a complementary session with one of the girls in exchange for overlooking the age restriction. Lauren still paid for the tattoo itself. In cash.

Eight:

One of the guys must stay at the girls' house each night, staying in Lauren's room. Reyna explained that it was for security. The guys had guns, although we rarely saw them, and they never talked about them. Half the time it was Bulldog staying overnight, and most of those nights Lauren stayed with him. When it wasn't Bulldog, then Blade or Shorty took over Lauren's room and used it for some of their wifey nights. On those nights, Lauren stayed at the guys' house. Lauren had pretty much taken herself out of the wifey dating pool, although there were a couple of times she and Shorty stayed together.

Nine:

Do not bring anyone to the house and do not tell anyone where we live.

Occasionally, one of the older girls would have a real boyfriend date with someone outside our group. Maybe a client she especially liked or maybe someone she met at a coffee shop. She would have to meet him somewhere public. One of the guys or Lauren would drive her to the meetup and pick her up later. They were strict about keeping clients and personal contacts away from where we lived.

* * *

Lauren no longer served clients unless she wanted to. She exempted herself since she was the business manager. But she had a few old clients she served at a higher price than the other girls. And I know a couple of times when one of the girls was out sick or on a recruitment trip Lauren stepped in for the scheduled clients.

Once Bulldog was free from babysitting me, I noticed he and Lauren spent a lot of time together. Bulldog and Lauren had wifey nights more often with each other than with others, which some of the girls grumbled about. Everyone liked Bulldog. I found out that Bulldog lost his virginity to Lauren when he was twelve and she was fifteen. I guess it was inevitable since they had been sharing a bed for a while. Lauren didn't even realize the irony of her anti-pedophile rule on her own past.

Bulldog and Lauren were almost like a couple. I say "almost" because they sometimes sleep with others. Like when Bulldog was with me or on big wifey dates. But they would often disappear together during the day. Reyna and Shorty were the next closest in their relationship, but not nearly as close as Bulldog and Lauren. They spent more time with each other than with others, but I got the impression Shorty was more into Reyna than she was into him. One sign was that Reyna still saw a lot of clients.

Once Lauren decided she needed more control of her situation, she and Bulldog would go out in the evenings to look for street girls who might be open to a partnership. Her selling point was that the girls would call the shots. She began to recognize some of the girls had similar tattoos, the brand marks of their pimps. Those girls were likely to be addicted to drugs and less inclined to hear Lauren's sales pitch.

Back then, Reyna was on her own and was more open to something that gave her security without sacrificing autonomy. She didn't want a pimp bossing her around. Although she was on her own regarding her work, she had a boyfriend: Shorty. He was an early client who began making repeated visits to blow the money he made working at a tire shop on her. She eventually moved in with him at his parent's house but continued to work the streets.

Lauren, Bulldog, Reyna, and Shorty formed a business alliance to look out for each other. That was after Lauren found out she wasn't wanted for murder, and long after she had turned eighteen. She arranged to rent a two-bedroom apartment for the four of them.

I call the four of them *the seniors*, as in, they are the senior members of the group. They are also the bosses. If I had to rank them, Lauren is number one, like the president or CEO. Bulldog is number two, and Reyna is a close number three. Shorty is number four. You might think Reyna and Shorty should be about the same rank since they joined at the same time, but Shorty just doesn't seem to have as much influence in decisions as the other three. Blade is sort of on the same level as the other girls. He's been there a while, but for a guy named Blade, I don't think he's sharp enough to be a leader. If we're still using business terms, he's more like an employee.

Escape Attempt

They moved me into the girls' house and put me in a room with Sarah. They probably paired me with her because she was also tricked into the business, so we had that in common. Sarah felt sorry for me and even apologized for my experience. I thought that was sweet and I immediately felt a bond with her. You know that old saying, "misery loves company." I certainly agreed with her complaints about our nighttime activity. The physical pain, the humiliation, the hopelessness. But then she continued to other aspects of life. So-and-so doesn't clean the bathroom well enough. We all eat too much junk food. Someone took her eyebrow pencil and didn't return it. Some of the girls don't take their clothes out of the dryer timely when she needs to use it. The quality of the toilet paper is bad. And since I mentioned toilet paper, the worst offense in Sarah's viewpoint, is that one of the girls puts the toilet paper on the holder backward. If I were to complain about the bathroom, it would be the lack of privacy, not toilet paper.

After a few days, I was tired of her complaints. I mean, sure, life sucked for both of us, so we had a lot to complain about. But eventually, even I wished she would dial it down.

At one point I complained to Kelly about Sarah's complaints.

"That's why they put you with her," Kelly said. "No one else can stand her."

Whereas Kanya was the most positive girl in the house, Sarah was the most negative. She was one of the reasons they delayed me moving into the girls' house. Sarah's old roommate wanted to switch and that made everyone else want to shuffle around, and it took a while to sort out who would room with who.

Kelly continued, "A few months ago, Sarah got under Reyna's skin so much that Reyna wanted to sell her to one of the gangs."

I thought she was pulling my leg.

"Seriously," Kelly emphasized, "she had a long discussion with Lauren about it. They were in Lauren's room with the door closed, but Nora and I still heard the conversation. Lauren vetoed it."

I was shocked that was even a consideration. But Kelly said it had a chilling effect on the girls like me who were tricked into the business. A lot of gang prostitutes never got out. They ended up strung out on drugs and eventually overdosed. At least, that's what Kelly said. From what I could tell, girls in our house could eventually graduate out. At least, my housemates sometimes mentioned those who had left under friendly circumstances, such as Eva, whose recent departure left a vacancy for me to fill.

* * *

The nightly sex sessions were bad enough, but the constant negativity from Sarah and the threat of getting sold to a gang just added to my woes. I oscillated between the fear and hopelessness of this new life – my second life – and the fear of my father's wrath if I could escape. A few days after moving into the girls' house the hopelessness of this life outweighed the fear of my father, and I tried to leave. I didn't even have to sneak. I just walked out one afternoon while everyone was busy doing their own thing. I didn't know where I was going. I just left with my backpack and a plastic garbage bag of clothes. Kanya saw me as she walked back from the convenience store at the edge of the neighborhood and intercepted my path. If I had been paying attention, I would have hidden, but from a distance, I thought Kanya was one of the neighborhood kids.

Kanya saw my bag and immediately knew what I was doing. "Are you trying to go back to your family?"

I had to admit I didn't know. Her question about family brought fresh doubt to my ability to confront my father.

"I don't think my parents would take me back."

Kanya ticked off my options. "One, you could go to a shelter. But they would get Child Protective Services involved, who might send you back to your parents or to a foster family. Just ask around the house; no one who had a foster family had a good experience. Some had dads or brothers who got a little too friendly with the girls, if you know what I mean. Some controlled every itty-bitty thing about their lives, even locking them in their rooms at night like jail. I could go on."

She went back to noting my options. "Two, you could live under a bridge and beg for money on the street corners like Kelly used to do. For a girl, that means you'd likely end up as the girlfriend of some old, bearded guy who hasn't bathed in forever or you'd get picked up by a gang. And," Kanya said, "gang pimps and homeless guys wouldn't treat you as nice as our guys."

I wasn't yet convinced about our guys being nice.

She added, "I like the wifey nights. The guys really care about us."

I told her, "They're just pretending to like you, so you'll make money for them. They're going to retire to mansions and you're going to end up on welfare."

"Well, they pretend very well," she defended. "And I'm going to college after I get my GED."

Last, she tried to gain my sympathy. "If you walk out, we'd have to move again," she said. "Like, tonight."

I was skeptical. "You're saying everyone would have to move out tonight if I left?"

"Yeah. That's what we did when April ran away a couple of years ago. We can't risk you telling the cops where we live."

"I swear I won't tell anyone."

"No one's gonna trust you about that." She tugged at my shirt sleeve. "Please don't leave. I just got my driver's license with this address, and I don't want to change it so soon."

The driver's license comment reminded me that she was eighteen. It was hard to think of her as an adult when she looked like a kid when she wasn't wearing makeup and despite the highlights in her hair and the tattoos, which were covered by a T-shirt at the moment.

She concluded her sales pitch by saying, "Staying is the best option for you. Even if you don't like it, it's better than the alternatives."

Trying to evaluate the odds of the various options, I asked, "Would they really sell a girl to a gang?"

"They did during my first year here. The girl just refused to fit in, and she tried to run away a couple of times."

"Do they ever let anyone just leave?"

"Of course. No one's gonna stay forever. Eva left a few weeks ago. Lauren helped her find a new place to live. You just need to put in your time here and eventually bring in someone else to join us."

Was I Kelly's recruit, her ticket to an eventual life beyond prostitution?

I decided to go back to the house with Kanya. Reyna saw us when we arrived. My bag of clothes gave away my intentions.

"Leaving?" she asked with raised eyebrows.

Kanya answered before I could. "She came back. That's what matters."

A few minutes later, Blade came over to the house and stood by as Lauren ordered me to the sofa in the living room.

"Lay down," Reyna commanded.

Everyone was staring at me, but I didn't move. Did they want Blade to rape me in front of everyone as punishment for trying to leave? I'd already been forced to have sex with 64 men – strangers – by this time, so rape by Blade didn't seem as terrifying as it once did. But maybe they thought doing it in front of an audience would add humiliation to the punishment.

Reyna nodded at Blade, and he picked me up and threw me face down onto the sofa. I started to turn over when he sat down on my butt. I twisted and struggled to get out from under him.

He growled, "Stop moving!" and slapped the back of my thigh for emphasis.

With my face-down position I knew it wasn't the rape I had expected, but I still didn't know what was going on. With Blade and several of the girls around me, I knew there was no point in struggling; I wouldn't be able to get away. I tried to look some of the girls in the eye, but each time, they averted their eyes. Only Reyna dared to stare back at me.

"You shouldn't have tried to leave," she said.

As the other girls stood around quietly watching, Blade pulled off my shoes and socks, then held my bare feet against the armrest, slightly apart. It was such a strange position.

Lauren started by tickling the bottom of my feet. Uncomfortable and humiliating. I thought the tickling was it. I couldn't help but try to kick my legs reflexively, but Blade just shifted to put more of his body weight on his arms as he held my ankles down.

Then a searing pain shot through my left foot. It was so unexpected and intense that I lost control and peed on myself and the sofa while yelling in pain. Lauren had hit the soft flesh between my heel and ball with a broken section of a fiberglass fishing pole that she used like a whip. After a few more whacks, she changed positions.

When I realized she was readying herself to exact her punishment on my other foot, I cried out, "I'm sorry! I made a mistake. I won't do it again!"

"I know you won't, Sweet Pea. But mistakes have consequences. They help you make better decisions later." Then she proceeded with my right foot.

When the torture was over, Blade stood up and I pushed myself up to a sitting position.

Reyna pointed to my pee-stained shorts and ordered, "Clean the sofa."

Lauren, Reyna, and Blade disappeared into Lauren's bedroom/office. I limped to the kitchen to get cleaning supplies, ignoring my wet shorts and the tears streaming down my cheeks, but Laney beat me to it and handed me a roll of paper towels and a spray bottle of disinfectant cleaner. I ripped off one sheet to wipe the pee from my legs and another sheet to wipe the tears from my face. I probably should have wiped my face first.

Laney quietly said, "They did that to me in my first week here. I should have warned you."

That night they made me take a roofie before work to make me relax. They didn't even try to trick me into taking it, just handed it to me with a glass of water. I remembered what they said about getting sold to a gang, so I took it.

That was also the night I started sleeping with Elena's penguin. Sometimes I talked to it, but only when no one else was around. I called it Elena because I imagined I was talking to the real Elena, telling her I wished I had run away to her house.

One good thing that came out of the escape attempt was that they put me with Kanya for a couple of weeks. Reyna ended up with Sarah. During that time, Reyna frequently told Sarah to "shut up" loud enough to hear from the other bedrooms. Reyna threw in some other words between "shut" and "up."

Kanya

On that walk back to the house with Kanya after my failed attempt to get away, I found out more about her.

Kanya's parents were Cambodian immigrants who used to be co-owners of a donut shop. They died in a fire when Kanya was seven. The business partner's family, the Kongs, also Cambodian, took her in. I don't even know Kanya's last name, but I can remember the Kongs because their name makes me think of King Kong. Like if King Kong had a family, they would be the Kongs. Anyway, at the time, they told her new elementary school that they were her parents. But they weren't. She was never formally adopted. Kanya worked at their donut shop from very early in the morning until it closed at noon. Then she cleaned the house and watched the Kong children after school and cooked for them in the evening. The Kongs kept her out of school after eighth grade, but she took some classes online. She was a fourteen-year-old domestic servant – a house slave – when she met the DollarFly girls.

"I never went anywhere, never did anything. If the Kongs took me with them, it was to babysit, not to play. The only friends I had were the guys at the donut shop, but they were all grownups. I'm not even sure they really count as friends. I wanted to get away so bad and do my own thing, take care of myself."

Several of the DollarFly girls visited the shop a couple of times a week. Their visits were in the late mornings when girls their age should have been in school. After a couple of visits, Kanya asked them what they did. Although they initially gave vague answers, they eventually told her they were models.

"I didn't believe them because models don't eat donuts. But they did have nice nails. One of the kitchen guys said he thought they were gang hookers because of the matching tattoos behind their ponytails. But they were nice. And they always put money in the tip jar."

Over the weeks, Kanya listened carefully to their conversations. She especially took note of their Tuesday morning visits, because the discussion often included some exciting event they did on Monday. She did not hesitate to interject herself into their conversation to ask them further about their lives, their living arrangements, how much time they had to themselves each day, and what they did for fun.

"Finally, I had enough of the Kongs. I still didn't know what the girls really did, but it had to be better than life with the Kongs. One morning, I came out from behind the counter and quietly asked if I could do what they did; if I could join them."

The girls gave her Lauren's phone number, and she called using a neighbor's phone. The next day, Kanya left the house when the family was out and walked to the edge of the neighborhood where Lauren picked her up with a couple of the girls she'd met at the shop.

"Lauren was skeptical of bringing me in after seeing how young I looked," Kanya said. "You know Lauren's rules about pedophiles, right?"

"Yeah. She told me we don't do pedos."

"Lauren said I look like a little kid, so it would be hard to keep pedos away when they saw my pics on the website. She didn't want me to join."

I found out two things from that statement. One, we were on a website. Remember that first day when Lauren had me do a photo shoot in Kelly's dress? Those photos were posted online so men could pick me. Two, Lauren and the group were picky and willing to turn down someone they didn't think would work out.

Rather than resort to deception with Kanya as they did with me, Lauren told her the truth. They *banged* men for money. Lauren thought that would dissuade Kanya from wanting to join them.

"I had to clean fish and butcher live chickens for dinner," Kanya told me. "It couldn't be worse than that."

But she didn't do those tasks multiple times every night.

Kanya confirmed with Lauren that what she'd heard from the girls over the weeks was true. Fun activities; date nights; a few hours a day to themselves. The girls with Lauren chimed in with examples of the fun activities: go-carts, laser tag, bowling, golf driving range, and even the Kemah Boardwalk.

"Lauren was giving the girls dirty looks when they were talking about that. I know Lauren was trying to talk me out of joining, but she didn't outright tell me I couldn't join."

"I had no life with the Kongs and I was tired all the time," Kanya told me. "I wanted to leave so, so, so bad, I didn't care if I had to *screw* strangers if I could have some time to myself." Then she added, "And have friends. These are the first friends I've had since my parents died."

Kanya was all in. The problem was that she looked twelve at the time. However, the other girls took a liking to her and convinced Lauren that they could do her makeup to make her look older.

Lauren had one last question for Kanya. "Have you ever had sex?"

Kanya told me Lauren closed her eyes and shook her head when Kanya told her, "No."

Lauren arranged to auction off her virginity and even let Kanya keep most of the money. The other girls insisted that Kanya get the final say in the auction buyer, even if it wasn't the highest bidder. After the bad experiences some of them – including Lauren – had, they wanted Kanya's first experience to be with someone she chose. Lauren agreed. Apparently, perverts are willing to pay big bucks for virgins, even those who are supposedly adults. I wondered how men would even know the girl is a virgin.

"The first thing I bought with the money was a smartphone." She sounded excited as she was remembering it. "I wanted one all my life, but the Kongs wouldn't let me have one, not even their old ones. I slept with that phone the first night I got it." Kanya held up her phone. "It's old now. Probably time for an upgrade."

She also got a cheap computer to take online classes. She was the only girl in the house interested in school. Lauren didn't trust me with a phone or a computer. She was probably afraid I would contact someone who would rat them out. Half of the girls don't have phones for that reason.

When I first met Kanya, I noticed she had a tattoo of a flying bird on her right shoulder. Later, when she wore a shirt that showed part of her back, I saw there was a tattoo of a bird cage with the door open on her right shoulder blade. The bird was flying away from it.

I felt like Lauren's group put me in a cage, but Kanya viewed the situation as freedom. How can one person see something as being so wrong, but others see the same thing as good?

Wifey Night

My first big wifey night was with Shorty, and I was afraid. My previous interactions with him weren't pleasant and his behavior with Blade was immature and sometimes aggressive. I don't know what Reyna saw in him. But the other girls assured me there would be no attacks and no roofies on wifey nights; the time was supposed to be enjoyable for both.

When he showed up at the girls' house, he was dressed nicer than usual. He wore a button-down shirt and loafers. He had shaved and smelled of cologne – the good kind in the right amount. Not like the boys in middle school who drenched themselves in it.

The whole night Shorty behaved like a gentleman. He opened doors for me and pulled my chair out at the restaurant. While we were there, I had to go to the restroom. I could have walked out of the restaurant and begged for someone to help me get away. But I didn't. I don't know why I didn't. Maybe Kanya was right, Shorty pretended very well. He was a better date than I was. I hardly talked the whole time, which forced him to do most of the talking.

After dinner, he took me to a workshop to paint ceramics such as vases or figurines. They had smocks for us to wear so we didn't get paint on our clothes. After you paint the items, the staff bakes them in a kiln to make the finish permanent and shiny. I chose a vase and painted flowers and vines on it. Shorty picked a statue of an eagle and painted it in weird colors, like orange feathers and a blue beak. I smiled at the absurdity. The absurdity of the eagle figurine and the absurdity of being on a date with my attacker and enjoying it. Then I was annoyed at myself for enjoying it.

One tradition of big wifey night is that the girl sleeps with her date. I'd already been forced with multiple men per night for several nights. At least this night would be only one guy. I lay there in Shorty's bed waiting for him to do his thing, but he merely kissed me and rolled over, away from me. I felt like I'd done something wrong. It's hard to explain the mixed feelings of hating him for what he did to me at the beginning, and then feeling rejected that he didn't want me on wifey night. I should have been relieved. I wasn't having some fantasy where the girl falls for the bad guy. I wasn't falling for Shorty. I just wanted to be wanted.

I woke up in the morning with his hand sliding between my thighs. Now that he wanted me, I would rather have gone without his further attention. At least he started with foreplay before climbing on top of me.

* * *

I had been with 94 men before that first big wifey night.

Shorty

Shorty was one of Reyna's clients in the early days when she worked the streets alone. His real name was Ezra. And he wasn't short. According to Reyna, his father was also named Ezra and when he was a kid, his uncles called him Shorty to distinguish him from his father. The nickname stuck.

When Shorty and Reyna met, he had just turned eighteen and worked at a tire shop during his senior year of high school. An uncle's birthday present to him was to pay for a hooker as a welcome to manhood. The uncle drove him to the part of town where hookers hung out and offered suggestions on which girls to choose. He even stopped an older prostitute and explained what he wanted for his nephew. The woman directed him to Reyna.

Shorty began blowing his paychecks from the tire shop on visits with Reyna. They hit it off well enough that she would see him when she wasn't working. About a year after they first met, she moved in with him at his parents' house.

She didn't stop turning tricks and Shorty didn't ask her to. But he did offer to look out for her. Clients behave better when they know the girl has a guy looking out for her.

When Reyna told Shorty about Lauren's proposal, he was more open to it than she was. It would mean getting out of his parents' house and their endless criticism of Reyna. Reyna thought it would be submitting to a pimp who would call the shots, impose quotas, and make her work when she didn't want to. Shorty just wanted to keep her safe.

While I think Shorty enjoyed wifey nights as much as the girls, I suspect he would be just fine if all his dates were with Reyna. I'm not sure Reyna felt the same way.

Shorty and Bulldog were the only ones in our group who still had family. That is, family that hadn't abandoned them. Bulldog only saw his mother once a year, but Shorty kept up with his family regularly. He and Reyna went to his parents' house for Thanksgiving and Christmas and his parents' birthdays. Sometimes he brought home a plate of homemade cookies or brownies that his mother baked for us.

On one of our dates, I asked, "Do you talk with your family about this business?" Of course, I mean prostitution.

"They know what Reyna and I do, but we avoid talking about it. If it does come up, we just say Reyna's a masseuse. That's like our secret code for the business."

"What does that make you?"

"Business manager."

Yeah, that's his preferred title anyway.

"They still harass my uncle about taking me out for my eighteenth, though." He smiled when he said the next part: "And my aunts wouldn't let him around my male cousins when they turned eighteen."

I envied him for having the possibility of a normal life. Unlike me or most of the girls, he could leave and go back to a regular job and a family who loved him. But I liked his mother's cookies.

The Complainer

My time as Kanya's roommate came to an end. Kanya and Kelly were supposed to be roommates, but Kelly had taken Reyna's bed while Reyna was rooming with Sarah. Reyna made it clear that she was tired of Sarah's attitude. According to Kanya and Kelly, Sarah was a complainer when she first joined the group but toned it down after the other girls told her to knock it off.

She had been with the group for a few months before I came. She despised what we did and didn't know how to get out. Her capture story was like mine, except that instead of complaining online, she complained in public. She had been in the foster system and hated the family she was with. Kanya was at a store and heard Sarah talking to someone on the phone about her life. Kanya told her our group helped girls like her and if she ever wanted to talk about it, we have people who could help. Kanya looks so young and innocent when she wasn't made up for work. She got Sarah's Instagram account and began messaging her. She introduced her to Bulldog via Instagram DM. Lauren accessed Bulldog's account and catfished Sarah as Bulldog. I don't mean to make Kanya sound bad because Kanya is a sweet person. She probably truly believed Sarah would be better off with us than with the family she hated. But not every family is as bad as Kanya's. And sometimes complaints have more to do with the complainer than the actual situation. Nevertheless, Kanya didn't tell Sarah what we really did, and Sarah took the bait.

Kanya got a recruiting bonus when Sarah came in. I have no idea what Kanya could spend it on since our living situation is pretty basic. She was old enough to live on her own and, supposedly, if she left on good terms, she could take the money with her. Later, I found out she was saving to buy a car.

If Sarah managed to get away, she would likely enter the foster system again. And with the runaway mark against her, it might be hard to find another family. She could end up with a family who thrives on abuse, knowing the kids have nowhere else to turn. Her suppressed unhappiness bubbled up when I came along. Maybe I should say 'boiled over,' because bubbles usually make people happy, and Sarah's bubbles didn't make anyone happy. Apparently, she viewed me as a new audience.

One night after work in November, we all piled into the trucks to go home. But Shorty and Reyna directed us all to squeeze into Bulldog and Blade's trucks. Except for Sarah. Reyna took the driver's seat of Shorty's truck and Shorty sat in the back with Sarah. We drove home and they headed downtown.

When they got to the house a couple of hours later, Sarah's shirt was covered in dried vomit. Reyna carried two cardboard boxes – the kind we keep our clothes in – inside the house and into our bedroom, then went to her own bedroom without saying a word. When she made eye contact with me, I got the vibe that talking to her would be dangerous.

Shorty said Sarah looked confused when they left the motel, but the panic set in when she noticed her boxes of belongings in the front seat. They expected a strong reaction, which is why Shorty sat in the back with her and let Reyna drive; he was more capable of restraining her than Reyna would be. When they got to the area where street hookers hung out and gang symbols tagged walls and fences, Sarah began screaming and thrashing about. When they stopped next to a guy who looked like a gang member and Reyna rolled down the window, Sarah threw up on herself and begged them not to sell her to a gang.

One rumor was that her terror softened Shorty's heart and he convinced Reyna to bring her back. The other rumor was they never intended to sell her, they just wanted to scare her. Reyna and Shorty wouldn't talk about it.

I'd only been there a few weeks. I hadn't cried in days, but I did that night. Not so much because of concern for Sarah, but because I realized that crossing the seniors could be devastating. I held Sarah for a long time that night and we both cried.

She avoided Reyna from then on and her complaining stopped, which was nice. But I noticed her alcohol consumption increased both before and after work. A lot more.

* * *

I'd been forced with almost two hundred men by this time.

Reyna

Reyna didn't like to talk about herself. But over several conversations with her and the other girls, I pieced together Reyna's background. Reyna's mother was a prostitute, and she never knew her father. In her younger years, she and her mother lived in a shabby apartment with another prostitute. I can't remember her name, but let's call her Jennifer. Reyna knew what her mother and Jennifer did for a living; she'd heard them talk about their work. With all the men the two women saw each night, they should have had a decent income, but they blew too much of it on drugs. A lot of hookers did that.

"My mother warned me many times not to follow in her footsteps," Reyna said. "She hoped I could be a dental hygienist or something like that." She snort-laughed, "That didn't work out.

"When I was in sixth grade, I had a crush on this boy who rode my school bus. His name was Mason. I watched him for months. He was sort of a rebel, throwing individual cooked green peas out of the window to splat onto car windshields. He and his friends always found something to laugh at. I don't know what they laughed at, but I liked his laugh. He was in eighth grade and sat in the back with the other big kids. Once, for the ride home I tried to sit next to him in the back. He and his friends teased me about being a little kid invading the big kids' rows. They kicked me back up to the front section. A few days later, I tried it again with a different strategy.

"I told him 'I'm gonna sit here and you're gonna see I'm not a little kid.' I took off my coat and spread it across our laps. And then I put my hand under the coat, on his lap."

I won't tell you what Reyna did next, but you can guess. I assume it was an activity she picked up from hearing her mother and Jennifer talk about their many dates.

"The boy didn't tease me about being a little kid anymore. A few days later, on one of the days my mother hit the streets early, I got off at his stop and went home with him. I started doing that more and more. One day, his mother came home early and found us together. After I put my clothes back on, she gave me a ride home and told me never to see Mason again or she would report me to CPS.

"The next day on the bus, I tried to save a seat for Mason, but he just shook his head and sat a few rows up. One of his eighth-grade buddies came and sat next to me. Mason must have told him what happened. He asked if I was ready to go back to the little kid section at the front of the bus.

"I told him, 'I'm not a little kid,' and he said, 'Prove it.' Then he pulled out a water bottle and as soon as he took the lid off, I could smell that it wasn't water. He said it was vodka. 'Drink some.'

"I wasn't sure how much I was supposed to drink. I took a few sips and made a face, then he laughed and took the bottle away. He put the cap back on and stuffed it in his backpack. Then he spread his jacket over our laps."

When Reyna was still in middle school, her mother was busted in a sting operation and ended up assaulting a cop in the process. She was hauled off to jail and forced into drug rehab. That meant she wasn't contributing to rent and food.

"Mom didn't tell them she had a kid at home. Maybe she thought I would be better off with Jennifer than in the system. But Jennifer wasn't happy to be stuck with me. After a few weeks, she said, 'I can't pay for this apartment and your food by myself.'"

Reyna snorted laughter again. "She could if she didn't blow all her money on drugs and alcohol, but I didn't tell her that. She said, 'You need to start bringing in some bucks or we're gonna be living under a bridge.' I was thirteen. It's not like I could get a real job. I borrowed one of my mom's dresses and went out with Jennifer. Grown men weren't like Mason.

"A couple of years later, I met Shorty. When I moved in with him, I was sixteen, but we told his parents I was eighteen. They weren't happy about the arrangement, but he somehow talked them into it."

Parking Lot Carnival

My birthday was January third. No presents, but I got homemade cards and a cake. I can't say I was surprised since we celebrated Laney's birthday similarly a few weeks back. Maybe our gift was the shortened workload they allowed us for one of the weekdays. On the designated birthday night – delayed if a weekend night – we got to leave the motel early with Lauren.

The cake said, "Happy 19th, Allie." That was an inside joke. Since clients are told that all of us girls are at least eighteen years old, that meant any birthday would be over eighteen. Some of the girls have had several 19th birthdays.

A few days later, Reyna announced that we were switching around our weekly fun day in celebration of my birthday. Not forever, just for that week. One of the seniors heard that a traveling carnival had set up business in the parking lot of a shopping mall across town and they decided that would be a nice diversion for us for the upcoming Sunday. We were still expected to work Sunday night, so it wasn't a totally free day like Mondays. They told us to take our changing clothes and makeup with us as we might have to go straight to the motel after our adventure.

Sarah asked if we still got Monday night off.

"Yes," Bulldog answered. "But we don't have anything planned. You can just do games or Netflix or something."

Do you know how hard it is to get nine girls to agree on a movie?

"I can finally watch Monday night football!" Blade interjected.

Kelly responded, "Not at our house."

Kanya surprised me with, "I'll watch it with you, Blade."

"Seriously?" Kelly asked rhetorically.

"I'll come too," Nora added.

So much for female solidarity. At least it would be easier to pick out a movie. Or maybe we could get a board game going. The others seem to like "Cards Against Humanity."

* * *

As we got out of our vehicles at the carnival I, for a moment, felt like a kid. The carnival had all the usual rides. Towers that dropped you, giant pendulums that swung you up and over, whirly rides that spun you in circles, and the usual carnival food: popcorn, cotton candy, and corndogs, the good kind made with beef. The weather was even cooperating. In early January in Houston, the temperature could range from 55 to 75 degrees. On this day, it was about 70.

I heard Lauren say, "Brings back memories, doesn't it?"

I thought she was talking about the carnival, but when I turned, I saw her looking at a recreational vehicle parked a few rows over. A young woman leaned against the side of the RV, chatting with a man a few feet away. Lauren had made her comment to Bulldog.

The others in our group had started toward the amusements, when Bulldog put a hand on Lauren's shoulder and said, "When we're done with this, I wouldn't mind traveling the country with you in one of those."

Lauren nodded, "Just us, no business."

Reyna turned back and pointed to the RV. "Check it out."

A man approached the woman at the RV and they both went inside. A few minutes later a different man exited the vehicle.

The others in our party came back, wondering why the seniors were still in the parking lot. After all, the seniors had the money for the ride tickets.

As we watched, another young woman came out of the RV and said something to the first man before she leaned against the vehicle near the door at the spot where the other woman had been leaning.

"Now it really brings back memories," Lauren commented.

Reyna said, "Y'all go ahead. Me and Shorty are gonna check it out. See if there's an opportunity."

Bulldog, Blade, and the other girls headed toward the carnival. Lauren and I moved closer to the RV, watching Shorty and Reyna.

"Why are you still here?" Lauren asked me. "Go join the others. We'll catch up later."

I was curious. Naïve me still hadn't figured out what was going on and I wanted to see what got Reyna's attention.

"It's okay. I'll wait with you," I told her.

In view of the woman at the RV, Reyna pulled out a wad of cash and handed it to Shorty.

"Take care of my horny cousin here," Reyna told the woman. "He's staying over at my place tonight and I don't want him getting all grabby like last time."

"Hey!" Shorty complained. "It's not like you're my sister."

"You may think it's funny, but I only tolerate you because we're cousins." She looked at the woman again and asked, "What's your name?"

"Raquel," she answered.

"Well, Raquel, I hope you can take care of him." She looked at Shorty and said, "Text me when you're done. I'll tell you where to meet us." Then she walked towards the carnival entrance.

I looked at Lauren in amazement. "They're hookers?"

She chuckled. "It took you long enough to figure it out."

* * *

We were waiting in line at a rickety roller coaster when Shorty joined us.

"How'd it go?" Reyna asked.

He grinned as he responded, "Well, I won't be getting all grabby with you tonight."

She rolled her eyes and said, "You know what I mean."

"They're not interested. Raquel said she and the other girl own the rig and her boyfriend – the guy standing outside –

comes along for moral support. It may be true, or it could be a load of *crap* that her pimp told her to say. I gave her your number anyway and talked her into putting it in her phone."

"Oh!" I exclaimed, just now getting it. Did I mention I was naïve? "It was a recruiting visit."

Lauren shook her head as if she was disappointed in me.

"Why didn't you get me to check 'em out?" Blade asked. "Next time I can do it."

"Because," Reyna tapped him on his chest, "last time you got caught up in the sex and forgot it was a recruiting mission. Wasted our money."

"You took it out of my pay," Blade pointed out.

Blade

Blade's real name was Blake. He gave himself the name Blade to sound tough. Kelly said the idea that he needed a pimp name came from a movie. She referred to him as Gator behind his back. The girls would laugh when she said that. I didn't get the joke.

Only a few months ago, long after I left the DollarFly girls, I watched an old movie called *The Other Guys* with Sophie and Ty. It had a scene where a guy became a pimp for college girls and gave himself the pimp name of "Gator." I laughed so hard when I saw that. I mean, the movie was funny by itself, but remembering that Kelly was using that name for Blade made it even funnier. I had to explain it to Ty and Sophie, but they didn't think it was as funny as I did. I wished I could tell Kelly that I finally got the joke.

Weirdly, I have some good memories during a period that I hated so much and wanted so badly to get away from. Is there something wrong with me?

Blade had been homeless when Shorty and Reyna found him. They saw Blade intervene when a couple of drunk guys were trying to pick up some girls coming out of a bar. The girls clearly didn't want to go with the guys, but the guys didn't seem to get the message. Blade pulled out a knife and waved it around in front of the men. It distracted them enough for the girls to run to their car. As the girls were driving away, they rolled down the car window and shouted "thank you" to Blade.

Blade lived in his car behind the bar. He was one of the homeless people who didn't seem to have a drug problem. Until a few months before that, he had lived with his single mother who did have a drug problem. After he and his mother couldn't pay rent, his mother ended up in a government-funded rehab program. He worked part-time as a cook, dishwasher, and busboy in a Chinese restaurant near the bar, but couldn't afford rent. He was walking to his car when he intervened for the bar girls.

Lauren and Reyna had been talking about needing another guy to help with their growing business. They wanted someone who had a protective instinct. And Blade needed a place to stay.

He started around the same time as Kanya. Kanya said Lauren and Reyna had several wifey dates with Blade when he first started as part of his training in how to behave on wifey nights. He wasn't experienced with girls at the time, not just regarding sex, but in general. Reyna was his first.

He's still a bit awkward in groups and tends to hang around Kanya more than anyone else on the Monday fun events. I thought it was either because they started at the same time or because Kanya tolerated his quirkiness better than the others. He could get loud when showing his irritation if he thought someone was cheating at whatever game or sport he was playing, be it cards, video games, or basketball in the driveway. And he could come off as creepy if you didn't know him.

I got some of my information about him from the other girls, and more while riding with him to one of our Monday events.

"Do you ever see your mother?" I asked him on the ride. One of the other girls in the truck turned to me and held her finger up to her mouth as if shushing me; as if I shouldn't ask that.

"I did at first. When she got out of rehab, she hooked up with a loser boyfriend who'd been supplying her with drugs. She was living with him and I didn't like being around him. They split up after a few months. I would've said that was for the best, but the next boyfriend wasn't any better."

The other girl looked at me and raised her eyebrows showing her surprise that he was talking.

Blade continued, "Then she moved around a bit and I lost track. Last I heard, she was living with a friend in some small town near Austin, working as a dog groomer. We never even had a dog growing up."

I decided to change the subject. "After Reyna asked you to work for them, what made you say yes?"

"At first, it was to have a place to live along with a job. It helped that Reyna was the best-looking girl who ever talked to me. She's like a 9 or 10 in my book. I think she was flirting with me.

"But if you want to know what keeps me here," he held up his hand and extended a figure for each of his points, "it's friends, a truck, and sex."

I nodded. What guy could turn that down? I wonder if sex was really the least benefit on his list.

"It's like I have eight girlfriends. Nine, if you count Lauren."

Yeah, sex was probably first on that list.

He added, "I like what I do here. I make sure you girls are safe. That's important."

I'm not sure if he is more protective of the individual girls or the operation as a whole because, amid his protection, he had no problem with using a cattle prod on an errant girl or holding her down for Lauren's beating. For the girls, that meant earning your keep and not trying to run away.

Kelly's graduation

Kelly was about the same age as Kanya but hadn't been with the group as long. After she turned eighteen, Blade helped her practice for the driving test. In February, a few months after she got her license, she announced she was going to live with Eva, the former DollarFly girl I replaced, and become a high-end escort where she would only have one client per night. Eva was getting a bigger apartment for the occasion.

Kelly had been with the group for more than four years. She started when she was fifteen after the seniors found her begging for money at a busy intersection. She ran away from a psychologically abusive mother and had been homeless for a couple of years, living in a tent with a homeless boyfriend twice her age. He was her second homeless boyfriend. The first was older than that. He had a seizure at a convenience store and was taken away by ambulance. When he didn't come back, she lived by herself for a few days until one of the others in the camp decided to take over the tent as well as Kelly. He offered her a modest amount of security. Modest in that other homeless men could not accost her directly; they had to go through him, her new boyfriend. For a pack of cigarettes, a bottle of wine, or a few bucks, they could get a few minutes alone with her. The payment was for the boyfriend, not Kelly.

Our group threw her a going-away party at a restaurant. It was our Monday Funday that week. One of her clients even came. He was the one who encouraged her to become an upscale escort. We helped her find bedroom furniture from thrift stores and garage sales that could be painted to look trendier. The girls also upgraded Eva's old living room furniture with new items from Ikea and Target. The guys helped her move and we girls helped her decorate. Lauren even gave them brand-new sets of dishes, glasses, cookware, and anything else she needed in the kitchen. And the dishes were the breakable kind, not the plastic stuff we used at the house.

One of my suspicions was confirmed at the going-away party. When Kelly introduced me to Eva, Eva commented to Kelly, "Oh, your replacement," before greeting me.

Although I filled the vacancy that Eva left when she moved out, Kelly was credited with recruiting me. She's the one who found my Instagram account and continued messaging me – as Bulldog – until she thought I was ready to meet in real life. I hadn't thought about the recruitment process since the time Kanya brought it up when I tried to leave. But the conversation with Eva dredged it up again. Kelly pretended to be someone else, sympathized with my situation, and acted as if she could offer me a better life. Not only did she pretend to be Bulldog, but she pretended to be a noble version of him, one that had my best interest in mind. Her DM exchanges didn't just provide an outlet for my complaints, her questions and statements were designed to feed my anger and soften me up to the idea of running away.

I had held a grudge against Bulldog and the other seniors since that first week, but pretty much thought of the other girls as either victims of the seniors or victims of their circumstances. Hearing the conversation between Eva and Kelly made me realize that any of the girls might be willing to victimize someone else to give themselves a way out. Kanya was credited with bringing in Sarah even though Kanya didn't seem to want to leave any time soon.

Would I become so desperate that I would be willing to betray an innocent girl into joining so that I could eventually leave? For the next few days, whenever I saw a girl around my age out in public, I wondered if I would be able to sell her out.

A few days later I was on a date with Blade, and I saw a girl at a restaurant – probably about fourteen or fifteen – arguing angrily with her parents. Heard her, actually. I think everyone in the restaurant did. She was angry that they didn't allow her to go somewhere with her friends and she accused them of being too controlling. I think half the teenagers in America have had a conversation like that. I know I did. At one point, she got up to go to the restroom and I decided to follow.

Inside the restroom, I commented, "Parents can be so difficult, can't they?"

"They hate me," she responded. "I don't think they ever wanted to have a kid and they take it out on me."

"That sucks."

"Well, I hate them, too."

"My parents sucked, too," I told her. She was seeing me as a sympathizer. This was my chance to introduce her to the dark side.

She finished her business and as she washed her hands, I said, "There are worse things."

"Like what?"

"I left home when I was sixteen. Now I *screw* fifty guys a week to have a place to stay and food to eat."

She stared at me open-mouthed while the water continued to run in the sink.

"If you think your situation is bad enough, I can put you up and show you the business."

She quickly left without drying her hands. I turned off her faucet. I didn't hear any arguments from her table for the rest of her meal. I'm not sure she talked at all. When the family got up to leave, the girl looked back at me. She was probably wondering if I had been joking. I gave her gave a little wave and she quickly looked away.

No, I didn't yet have what it takes to bring in a vulnerable girl. Nevertheless, I pictured little drops of my soul getting left behind with each sexual encounter, carried away as stains on the clothes of the men who were so eager to use me each night. Eventually so little of my soul would remain that I would view a vulnerable girl as prey rather than as a person.

Is that what happened to Kelly and Kanya? Or did their souls begin leaking out before they became DollarFly girls?

The other thing I learned from Kelly's exit is that I have choices for my future. I don't have to become a stripper. I could instead become an escort.

* * *

The morning after Kelly's party, as I headed to the kitchen, I saw Nora standing at the doorway to Lauren's bedroom.

"Hey Lauren, Kelly's party got me thinking."

"That sounds dangerous," Lauren said.

"I'm nineteen now. I'd like to …."

Lauren interrupted her with, "You know you have to find a replacement."

Final confirmation of my suspicion that finding a replacement was a criterion for being allowed to leave the group.

"I know, but once I find one, could I …."

Lauren interrupted her again with, "Come in and close the door."

As I was preparing my breakfast of cereal and orange juice, Nora came out from Lauren's room, red-faced and frowning.

"What is it?" I asked.

"Apparently I haven't *screwed* enough men yet!"

She'd been with the group for about two and a half years.

* * *

By the end of February, I had been forced with over 800 men. How much of my soul leaked out with each client? And how much of it would be gone by the time I screwed enough men?

-Review Session Two-

Amanda handed Alia the assignment draft with her markups.

"I pictured sex trafficking as that movie, 'Taken,' where the girls were kidnapped, locked up, and drugged up. Maybe with a tattooed man guarding the door while smoking a cigarette."

Alia nodded at the stereotype. "Yeah, that may happen to some girls, but my situation was different."

Amanda sighed. "I think back to seeing groups of girls at the mall or the movie or somewhere and now wonder if they could be part of a prostitution ring."

"I'm not sure I would even be able to tell," Alia said. "Maybe if there were a couple of older guys – or girls – with them, I might be suspicious. But that's the strategy for not getting caught. When we weren't at a motel, no one would know what we were."

"You were brainwashed."

"That's what Ty said."

"It's hard to believe they would just let a girl like Kelly leave."

"You make enough money for the seniors, find a replacement, and when you're old enough, you can go. No hard feelings. I think in some messed up way, Lauren actually believed she was doing a good thing."

"Taking advantage of vulnerable girls is not doing a good thing," Amanda noted. "I feel sorry for her for all she went through, but that doesn't make it right to push it onto other girls."

Alia handed Amanda another stapled set of papers.

"Honey, how much more do you have after this?"

"Oh, I'm sorry. I know it's a lot of trouble. Maybe I can get someone else to review it."

"That's not what I meant. I made a commitment and I'm sticking to it. It's just a lot of dark stuff to read about."

Amanda slapped her knee and sat up straighter on the loveseat. "I'm implementing a new rule for these visits."

Alia raised her eyebrows.

Amanda continued, "We have to talk about something fun and lighthearted before I read the serious stuff. Are you still seeing that boy at A&M?"

"Andy. Yes, we're still dating."

"Good. I live vicariously through my kids. Anna doesn't call me enough, so you have to keep me entertained. Tell me about your dates with Andy. Does he treat you right?"

Alia smiled at the thought. "Yes. He treats me right. That's what I love about him. He knows what I was, and it doesn't matter to him. Last Friday, I skipped school and went to the rodeo with him. Chapel Heart was playing."

"Now that's the kind of delinquency I can get on board with. Tell me more."

After their visit, Amanda walked Alia to the door to see her off and restated her commitment to review Alia's paper until the end. "Alia. I'm glad you found us. If Ty and Sophie ever give you trouble, you're welcome here." She put an arm around Alia's waist. "I have to give you one more hug before you leave."

Alia smiled as she leaned in.

The Twins

One Saturday morning in March, Bulldog and Kanya left together. It was common for Bulldog and Lauren to go off together, but not Bulldog and one of the girls. We don't do wifey dates on Saturdays, so it wasn't that.

Monday, they returned with two girls. At least, we could tell the Hispanic kid with shoulder-length hair was a girl even before being introduced. Her name was Catalina. However, with short box braids, plastic-rimmed eyeglasses, and baggy clothes, the gender of the Black kid was harder to tell. Even after Bulldog introduced the kid as Kennedi – or was it Kennedy? – we weren't sure. Is Kennedi a girl's name or a boy's name? Maybe it could be either. Fortunately, Kanya's reference to her as "she" provided some assurance. When she opened her mouth to greet us, we were once again left dumbfounded. She had braces.

When Lauren saw Kennedi, she just about lost her crap. Kennedi looked like a kid. And at thirteen, she still was one. A kid with acne and braces. While Kanya introduced Catalina and Kennedi around the house, Lauren pulled Bulldog outside and chewed him out for bringing someone so young. I hung out in the front bedroom – what used to be a formal living room – to watch Bulldog and Lauren through the window and hear their conversation, listening for clues as to the circumstances of the girls' recruitment.

"Maybe we can use her as bait to lure all the pedos!" she yelled. "Then you can hold 'em down while I chop their *peckers* off! Or did you forget about our no pedo rule?!"

Bulldog made excuses that it was either both girls or neither and since they already invested time and money in Catalina, he decided to accept both.

"I don't want clients thinking they're getting a kid!" Lauren scolded. "How can she pass for an adult?"

"You can work your makeup magic," Bulldog answered defensively, raising his voice to match Lauren's.

"And those damn braces? We can't take her to an orthodontist without raising suspicion."

"We'll think of something," he replied again. "You're good at that." He tried to kiss her, but she turned her head.

That was the end of the conversation. I could hear the front door open and close. Then it opened and closed again. Lauren had come inside and closed the door in Bulldog's face before he could follow her in. She went to her room and closed that door in Bulldog's face, too. She didn't lock it, though, so Bulldog went in after her. Their conversation was quieter after that, so I couldn't hear them.

I joined the group showing the new girls around. They were discussing tonight's activity of Bumperball, which was sort of like lacrosse in bumper cars, according to the others who were talking over themselves in trying to explain the odd sport. I had never heard of it.

In a few minutes, Lauren joined us, but not to make idle conversation. She stood in front of Kennedi, hands on hips, and stared at her, frowning. Kennedi looked at the floor.

After a few seconds, Kennedi raised her head and said, "I know I won't be a model. I already told Doug I can wash dishes and clean the bathrooms and vacuum the floors. You don't even have to pay me. I'll do anything to stay."

It had been so long since I had heard Bulldog's real name, it took me a moment to remember that Doug was Bulldog.

Of course, if she knew what we "models" really did, she wouldn't have said that. As much as I liked the idea of having someone do our chores for us, I wanted to warn her, to tell her to get out while she could. I was seventeen and still sometimes got sick to my stomach about what I did. She was just a kid.

But I didn't say anything. I couldn't. I knew they couldn't let her leave, or she could expose the whole operation. So, if I said anything, it would just bring the wrath of the seniors and a few long-timers on me. One of the milder forms of punishment would be to give me all the worst clients, the ones no one wanted. The crushingly overweight men, the smelly ones, the ones with oversized equipment, and the ones who like to get rough with the girls. So, I held my tongue.

Kennedi spoke again. "I don't even have to do the game tonight. I can just watch everyone's stuff."

Lauren inhaled deeply and exhaled a heavy sigh. She took Kennedi's hand and said, "Come with me, Sweet Pea. Let's go for a ride in Quick Sadie." Quick Sadie was Lauren's nickname for her white Infinity QX80. It was the same vehicle Bulldog and

Kanya drove to Austin to get Cat and Kennedi. Lauren thought recruits would be more impressed with the Infiniti than a pickup. She led Kennedi toward the door to the garage.

The rest of us had already frozen at Lauren's stare-down, but now we exchanged glances and Lauren noticed our concern. "Oh, come on!" she said. "I'm not Cruella. I'm taking her shopping. If she's staying here, we can't let her wear sweatpants all the time."

Catalina

During the afternoon, I sat down with Catalina to get her story. I wanted to find out if she knew what she was getting into or whether she was deceived like me. Reyna stayed close by. I suspect she was there to make sure I didn't give away any secrets.

Catalina was fifteen. I found that her connection was through a former DollarFly girl, Rachel, who had left the group before I came. Kanya said Rachel worked as a stripper in Austin and made adult videos that she posted to an online subscription service. There's another career possibility for me.

Catalina met a guy named Jason at a shopping mall before Christmas. She was with her foster siblings and wasn't very happy to be there. Jason was standing nearby and made some joke about her looking miserable. She didn't remember exactly what he said, but they talked for a few minutes while the others argued about where to go next. Just a brief, casual conversation between strangers. She didn't engage further and he didn't push it, but during their brief conversation, she gave him her name.

"After Christmas, I saw Jason again at a department store. He called my name and asked how my Christmas was. I couldn't believe he remembered my name. It was kind of nice, you know?

"I told him Christmas was just 'Meh, nothing special.'

"Then Rachel came up and hugged Jason. He introduced me to Rachel as if he and I were old friends. Rachel said she had more shopping to do. 'It was good seeing you, Jason. Call me; I might have a photoshoot for you. See you around.' Then she told me, 'Nice to meet you, Catalina. I'll leave you and Jason to your shopping.' She thought Jason and I were together."

Catalina didn't know Jason was Rachel's boyfriend and that they lived together. Bulldog told me that later.

It sounded like Catalina was a little more open with Jason after the Rachel encounter. They chatted more while her family shopped. She explained she was at the store with her foster family. Christmas was disappointing. The family has too many kids and the parents don't pay enough attention to them. She said they foster for the money rather than because they love children. The government gives them a monthly stipend for each kid they foster. Jason and Catalina began connecting through Instagram.

I asked her about her family. Like, what did they think of her joining our group? Of course, I knew she didn't tell them. That's not how this works. But I wanted to hear her explain it.

"I wanted nicer clothes. I mean, I wasn't wearing rags, but I wanted something better than what they sell at Walmart. They get government money for being foster parents. But they also get donations from random people. They don't want us to look too good because they think looking poor gets them more donations. I was hoping they would be a little less stingy for Christmas.

"That's just an irritation. What really gets me is that they don't pay attention to us. The younger kids get all the attention and we older ones get crickets. They don't even pay attention to their biological kids. Not even when one kid picks on another. Sometimes I just want acknowledgment; maybe ask how I'm doing; maybe tell me 'Good job' when I get a good grade. I felt more like a tenant than a family member."

That's where the connection with Jason came in. They continued chatting through Instagram direct messages. Her dumb granny phone couldn't load apps, but she could get to Instagram from a computer.

"Jason would ask me how my day went, and how was school. If I got an "A" in school, he would congratulate me. He also told me I was photogenic. He was a photographer, so he would know. That was nice. The fosters never gave me compliments.

"Then Jason invited me to meet up at the park in my neighborhood where he was doing a photoshoot with Rachel, the girl I met at the store when I ran into Jason. He took some photos of me, too, and posted them to his Instagram account. I downloaded copies for myself. He made me look better than I really look. Then he drove us to a coffee shop. It was cool to hang out with grownups.

"Rachel gave me her old phone so I could talk with her or Jason if I was ever feeling down. I had to hide it because my foster parents thought I was too young to have a smartphone. I'm fifteen! Everyone else at school had a smartphone for years.

"One time, we all met at the coffee shop. I brought Kennedi for that one because a couple of the boys at home were giving her a hard time and she needed a break. They can be mean sometimes. And it's not like our foster parents would do anything to stop it. Another time, Rachel invited me to a fashion photoshoot with her and Jason. We went to her apartment, and she posed in different outfits and jewelry. We drank wine and did shots. They treated me as an equal. Then Rachel did some lingerie photos, including a topless pose.

"I wish I was that confident. I did pose for some photos, but not like hers. Just some lame fashion shots with her jewelry. She even let me take some of her jewelry home.

"Jason said he would give me the photos when we met again."

Rachel told Catalina about the modeling agency in Houston that she used to work for and said she thought Catalina would be a good fit. She spoke of the fond memories of the girls and some of the social activities they did, including date nights with the guys. No one was ignored. Rachel connected her with Lauren and Bulldog. They talked via FaceTime on Rachel's phone. Bulldog visited Austin one Saturday afternoon and met Rachel, Jason, and Catalina for lunch at an upscale restaurant. Rachel bought Catalina a new outfit before lunch, something more suitable for the restaurant.

"We went back to Rachel's apartment after lunch to continue chatting. I said I needed to change back into my old clothes before going back home. Doug said, 'Tell them a friend gave you her used clothes that she didn't want anymore.' Then he looked at Rachel and asked, 'Rachel, do you want them?'"

She said, 'Not anymore.'"

Catalina laughed as she recalled that scene.

"I thought they were kidding," she said, "but Rachel took off her clothes and told me to give her the new clothes I was wearing. She was just standing there in her underwear in front of Doug and Jason. She'd done that before for a photo shoot, so maybe it shouldn't be so surprising. I guess that's normal for you models."

Yeah, that was my initial thought when Kelly let me borrow her dress on my first day.

"Jason went to the kitchen to fix us drinks and Doug and Rachel just stood there, waiting for me to do something. Then Doug asked, "Do I need to turn around?"

"And Rachel said, 'You've already seen everything there is to see of me, but why don't you turn around for Cat.'

"He turned around and I took off the blouse and gave it to Rachel and she put it on. Then I took off the jeans and handed them to her and she put her feet in and pulled them up to her thighs. She began laughing and said, 'That's about as far as they'll go,' which made Doug turn around to see what she meant. He started laughing, too.

"He saw me in my underwear, and I felt kind of awkward. He must have noticed – I mean I know he saw me, but I mean he must have noticed me looking awkward – because he said, 'Sorry,' and turned back around.

"Rachel gave me back the clothes and I put them on as fast as I could. I was embarrassed, but I was also embarrassed for being embarrassed. Rachel had no problem changing in front of him. He was cool and easy to talk to at the restaurant. I wanted him to like me. But I'd just met him in person and it's weird to get undressed in front of someone you barely knew.

"Rachel said, 'Now the clothes are used. So, if anyone asks about your new clothes, you can tell them your friend gave you her used clothes that she doesn't want anymore. Especially because the jeans don't fit.' She turned to Bulldog and added, 'I'm so smart. Oh, and you can look now.'

"Rachel is kind of funny. We stayed a little longer and drank wine and Doug, Jason and Rachel talked about world events."

Bulldog and Kanya drove to Austin again and met Cat for lunch that Saturday. Catalina goes by 'Cat', but Kanya dubbed her 'KittyCat', and later just 'Kitty'. Bulldog and Kanya also treated that night as their wifey night.

Cat continued, "I like Kanya. Saturday, she was dressed up and had on makeup, and looked all grown up. But Sunday, she wore regular clothes, no makeup, and she looked younger than me. She told me about life with the agency."

That was the first time I heard our group called an agency. She asked, "Are Kanya and Doug a couple? They slept in the same bed last night, and she even went into the bathroom to brush her teeth while he was taking a shower. It was the kind with a glass door, so she would've seen everything."

When Bulldog first brought me to Houston, we arrived late and came directly to the guys' house, but last night he took Cat and Kennedi and of course Kanya (that's a lot of "K" sounding names), to a nice hotel by the Galleria. I knew they were trying to avoid meeting us as we prepared for work. It would raise too many questions that he would rather deal with later. And maybe he was still trying to impress Cat and Kennedi, the Twins.

In answering her question, I decided to tease her a bit. "Did the room have two beds?"

"Yeah."

"And you slept with Kennedi while Bulldog slept with Kanya?"

"Yeah."

"Would you have rather slept with Doug?"

She turned red. "No, that's not…"

I interrupted before she could finish. "It's Kanya, isn't it? You have a thing for Kanya. It's okay. We all do."

"No, no, no. I'm not like that. They just seem like a couple."

Maybe I took the joke too far with someone I just met. I looked at Reyna before I explained, "They're not a couple. I've slept with Doug, too." Reyna frowned and gave a little shake of her head to indicate her displeasure at the direction of our conversation. "So has Reyna. We all have." I thought Reyna's eyes were going to pop out of her head.

Cat looked shocked and maybe a little skeptical, not knowing if I was kidding or not. "We're all very close here." Reyna gave a slight nod at that.

I took that segue to ask Cat if she had a significant other.

"No."

"Never?"

"We broke up a few months ago."

"Let me guess. Your parents found out, didn't approve of him, and told you to never see him again."

"My fosters didn't notice and probably wouldn't have cared if they did. They never seemed to care about anything I did."

"So, what happened?"

Cat squirmed at the question. I know Lauren doesn't want virgins as she believed they put up more resistance to our work. I was trying to gauge whether Cat was an exception to that rule.

"After he told someone about doing it with me in the back of his mom's minivan, I dumped him. You just don't share private stuff like that."

I agreed that she was right to dump him. Then I pulled the conversation back to the past weekend. Cat went on with her story of how she ended up with us.

"Saturday afternoon was good. Our time at lunch was such a big difference from how my family treated me. I mean, I felt like a person. As if people liked having me around. They invited me to come to join them in Houston. They said the Director had seen the photos Jason took of me and already agreed to accept me."

She was referring to Lauren. That's the first time I heard anyone call her a director, but the title fits. The part about *accepting* her was somewhat humorous. The criteria for us girls to be accepted were basically to be pretty and stupid. But I kept that to myself.

"I asked about the application process and permission form and Doug said they were very informal. If I wanted to go, they would take me.

"That night at dinner with the family, I guess I was being a little grumpy. I tried to start a grown-up conversation about current events, and they kept changing the subject to whatever they wanted to talk about. That's when I snapped and told them, 'No one pays attention to me around here.'

"My foster dad said, 'If you think you can find something better, go ahead.' Right there at the dinner table, I made my decision to leave. That night, I used Rachel's old phone to text Doug that I was ready. We arranged to meet at the park on Sunday. Yesterday."

Kennedi saw Cat packing and begged to go with her without knowing where she was going. She threw some belongings in a garbage bag and followed Cat. Cat was concerned about drawing attention if she argued with Kennedi, so she let her follow. It would be up to Doug to tell Kennedi that she couldn't come. Cat showed up at the park with Kennedi and neither one knew what they were getting into.

Later, I asked Kanya how that went down. Kennedi was a thirteen-year-old girl with acne, braces, and eyeglasses, who favored baggy clothes. According to Kanya, Kennedi said she knew she wasn't model material, but said she could be the maid. She was begging. Kanya said it was sad.

"We had a little meeting out of earshot of Cat and Kennedi," Kanya said. "Rachel pointed out the possibility that if we didn't take Kennedi, she could tip off authorities about

Cat's disappearance. So, we either had to leave both of them or take both of them."

And I'm sure Rachel and Jason wanted their recruitment fee. I don't know how much Lauren and Bulldog pay for recruiting someone, but it sounded like they didn't pay the full price for Kennedi. Lauren didn't know about Kennedi until they showed up that morning.

Kennedi

While I was talking with Cat, Blade left to buy another mattress and the bedding that went with it.

When Lauren drove off with Kennedi in the afternoon, we all thought the worst, despite Lauren's statement about taking her shopping. I hoped she wasn't dumping her somewhere or selling her to a gang. When they came back a few hours later, I thought Lauren had ditched Kennedi and picked up someone else. The passenger stepped out of the car wearing a designer minidress and high wedge sandals. She also carried a Macy's bag.

Lauren whispered something to her, and the young woman straightened her back to stand a little taller.

"Meet Kandi," Lauren announced, waving her hands toward the girl.

The girl smiled broadly at that introduction. That's how we knew it was still Kennedi. We saw her braces when she smiled. The biggest change was the makeup. Lauren must have paid someone a lot to work her in for a professional makeover. Her acne was gone – or at least covered – and the lipstick, eyeshadow, and eyeliner made her look glamorous and older. Then I realized she wasn't wearing her glasses.

Lauren whispered something in her ear and Kennedi – I mean Kandi – changed her grin to a closed-lip smile and tilted her head. She might pass for an adult with a few more accessories. If you saw her in a bar wearing stilettos and holding a wine glass, maybe with a small purse nearby, you probably wouldn't think *kid*.

Lauren had Kennedi/Kandi go around to the driver's side and pose by the open door while holding the car keys. Yep, that's an accessory that would make you think *adult*. Lauren took a couple of photos with her phone.

Monday night fun night. Everyone dressed for comfort but Kennedi. She didn't want to change out of the dress. But Lauren made her switch her shoes for sneakers.

* * *

Since Cat and Kennedi didn't already have a close relationship with one of the guys – like I thought I had with Doug/Bulldog – Lauren put them together in the big room with Lexi, aka Alexandra. That was the former living room that Lexi had shared with Kelly. Lexi was another one who was tricked into joining the group, but she'd come to terms with the situation.

Lexi

Lexi was seventeen and wasn't much of a talker, but if you got her alone, she opened up. Two years earlier, Blade and Eva – the girl I replaced – were cutting through a neighborhood on one of their wifey dates and found Lexi sitting alone in a park. Eva saw her wipe her eyes and told Blade to stop the truck. Lexi's single mother had been working nights and her father wasn't in the picture. Her older brother and his girlfriend frequently teased Lexi about being a loser. The girlfriend and their friend group made a practice of getting Lexi drunk for their entertainment and encouraged the guys in their group to molest her for laughs. It eventually progressed to full-on rape. That added to her depression. When Eva and Blade found her, she was pondering what would be the best way to end it all.

Eva sat on the grass in front of the bench and talked to Lexi for a while, mostly listening, while Blade sat on a playground swing several feet away. Eva invited Lexi to go get ice cream with them. She declined to get in a vehicle with strangers, so Eva sent Blade off to bring back ice cream. A half-hour later he came back with three vanilla ice cream cones in a cardboard carrier. Blade sat next to Lexi on the bench. Eva continued to sit in the grass.

Eva told Lexi about the home for displaced teens where she and Blade lived. Once they'd finished their cones, the afternoon had given way to evening, and Blade and Eva walked her home, leaving Blade's truck at the park. When she saw the cars of her brothers' friends parked in front of her house, she asked Eva and Blade if their home for displaced teens was real. When they confirmed it, she asked them to wait outside. She returned with a small suitcase, and they brought her to our group.

Even though her initiation was similar to mine, Lexi said she likes our DollarFly group much better than her brothers' friends, as no one makes fun of her, and the people here even provided encouraging words when she needed them most. She added that the house guys treat her well on wifey nights as if she matters. She knows they're not real boyfriends but said she's not sure she would be able to tell the difference. She even said our work, which she would rather not do, had its positive side. She felt she had value since men paid to spend time with her. And having repeat clients make her feel she's doing something right. It's a messed-up way of looking at this nasty business: screwing lots of strangers with encouragement is better than being forced to screw acquaintances under harassing ridicule.

We realized later that Lexi was a good choice to be a roommate for our new recruits.

Reality

Tuesday night was our work night. Cat and Kennedi watched us put on our evening makeup and then rode with Bulldog to the motel to see what our business is about. I didn't see their reaction because I was working. When Blade arrived after his little wifey night with Laney, Lauren finished up with a client and took Cat and Kennedi home early.

Wednesday was interesting. Lauren joined Lexi, Cat, and Kennedi in their bedroom. Cat was crying and repeatedly saying she wanted to go home. I tried to go into their bedroom, too, but Lauren sent me out and I saw her sit next to Cat on her bed before Lauren had Lexi close the door. I hung around the hallway to hear how they handled it.

Kennedi's reaction was surprisingly calm. She just asked questions about the operation. "Do the customers come to the house?"

Lauren answered, "No. Customers don't know where we live. We keep work separate from our personal lives."

"Do Doug, Shorty, and Blade come to the house and do stuff to you?"

This time Lexi answered. "They have keys to the house and can come over whenever they want. Sometimes they come over and eat with us and sometimes our Monday Funday is just to hang around here as a group – us and the guys."

Kennedi clarified, "I mean, do they come to your rooms and do stuff to you?"

"They don't come to our rooms," Lexi said, "unless we need them to fix a light or something. I'm not sure what you're getting at."

Kennedi further clarified, "Do they come to your rooms and touch you and stuff?"

"No," Lexi answered. "But on big wifey night – out big date night – we stay with them in the guys' house."

"All of them?" Kennedi asked.

"Only the one we're having a date with that night."

"Like Kanya and Doug slept together at the hotel?"

"If you're asking if we have sex with our guy, the answer is yes. Big date night is our wifey night."

I was still amazed at Kennedi's calm while Cat cried. By the questions she was asking, I felt she understood the situation, but maybe her naivete prevented her from understanding how it would soon impact her life.

"What's a wifey?" Kennedi asked.

"Like I'm the wife for a night. It doesn't feel like working. It's like we're a couple."

"And you know when it's gonna happen?" Kennedi asked.

"Yeah, it's scheduled. If you want to get with one of the guys at a different time, you can arrange it with him. Sometimes Lauren gets with Bulldog during the day."

That prompted Lauren to jump back into the conversation. "That's not just for *effing*. We usually just need to take care of business."

"*Effing* business." Lexi had a teasing tone in her voice.

Lauren replied, "I told you my story last night. I've known Bulldog since we were kids. We do a lot of things together besides *eff*."

I didn't tell them about my initiation. I assumed there would be sexual encounters with the guys before they put the new girls to work. Lexi previously told me that she stayed with Blade for the first couple of days. I also want to clarify that although the guys usually only have sex with us on the big wifey night, they could get a quickie at the motel during slow periods between clients. It wasn't very often, and Blade seemed to do it more than Shorty and Bulldog. In fact, I don't think I'd ever heard of Bulldog doing it. Blade seemed to visit Kanya more than anyone else.

Kennedi continued her inquiry: "Is wifey night really like a date? Like, you go out and do something fun? Or were y'all lying about that?"

"We go out on a real date," Lexi said. "We might even hold hands. You can suggest what you want to do."

Lauren decided this was a good line of questioning to distract them from discussing our nightly business. "What would you like to do on a date?"

"I don't know. Maybe eat at Chili's and go to a movie or a concert."

"Those are good ideas. What about you, Catalina?" Lauren asked.

Cat's delay in answering gave me the impression she was reluctant to participate in the conversation. Finally, she said, "I was hoping to go to Fiesta Texas with this boy from school, but never got to."

"Well," Lauren hesitated, "Fiesta Texas would be an overnight trip from here. You may have to wait on that one. But the Kemah Boardwalk is possible. It's not on the same level as Six Flags, but it's fun for a few hours."

Kennedi brought the conversation back to business. "One night a week is the Monday fun night and another night is a wifey date night. So the hotel nights are five nights a week. Right?"

Lauren answered, "That's right. Well, Monday night is a non-work night. We usually go out, but sometimes we do something at home like games or movies."

"One time we had a dance party in the den," Lexi added. "And sometimes the older girls do their own thing."

Cat finally pulled herself together to join the conversation. "Kennedi, you realize they're making us be prostitutes, don't you? Why are you asking all these dumb questions that don't matter?"

"I want to know," Kennedi stated plainly.

Cat wasn't finished. "How many men do you *screw* each night?"

I don't know if Cat was asking about us girls in general or Lexi or Lauren specifically. Lexi fielded that question. "Maybe ten. Sometimes more, sometimes less. Weekends are busier than weekdays."

I heard Lauren soften her voice and use the nickname Kanya had come up with. "KittyCat, your life sucked before. That's why you left. What we got here is not as bad as you think." I imagined Lauren rubbing Cat's back as she said that.

It's not as bad as being a gang hooker. We're not strung out on drugs and walking the streets, getting into cars with strangers who could be serial killers, getting beat up by our pimps for not making quota. At least, that's what the older girls said was the life of gang hookers. Our *managers* – remember, they don't like to be called pimps – are the ones setting up the appointments, so quotas are their business.

But it's still bad. It's just that we get desensitized to it after a while. First is denial. "This can't be happening to me. I'm not like that." Then comes anger. Angry at the seniors. Angry at my father. Angry at myself for messaging a stranger. Unresolved anger is what nearly got Sarah sold. Then sadness and depression hit. That's when alcohol consumption increases. I said we're not strung out on drugs, but I suspect some of us are alcoholics. Finally, the acceptance. "I am a prostitute." By the time Cat and Kennedi came, I'd probably had sex a thousand times.

We are prostitutes. We can't deny it. I thought my old life sucked, too. But that life was better than this. Except now I'm not afraid that someone's going to hit me in a fit of anger. Because now I try to be a good little girl; stay in my lane; make the customers happy. Too bad I didn't learn that before running away. The strange thing is that I feel more of a connection with this group – even with Shorty and Blade – than I did with my own father. And I get to wear stylish clothes.

After thinking for a while, Kennedi spoke up again. "Cat, I don't want to go back." Then she asked Lauren, "If none of the customers want me, can I still stay here? I can do all the chores."

"Sweet Pea," Lauren said gently, "I'm not sending you back. And we're not going to worry about clients right now."

* * *

When Lauren finally came out of the bedroom, I stopped her and asked, "Are you going to make the guys initiate them like they did me?"

Lauren had the nerve to ask, "Are you still pissed about that?"

"Yes."

"I'm open to suggestions. How do you think we should get Cat ready?"

"At least I'd already been with Bulldog when I got here. They haven't been with any of them."

"What's your idea?"

I hadn't formulated a plan; I just knew I didn't like what they did to me. "No ambush attacks. Let them do three wifey nights in a row – one with each guy – before making them see clients."

"The other girls might take issue with using up their wifey nights. And if we just wait for the weekly wifey nights, it'll take too long. We ain't a charity. We have bills to pay. Besides, would a row of wifey nights have made you more agreeable?"

"No. But maybe less angry."

"How would you keep Cat from sneaking away during one of those dates and having the cops raid us and toss you and everyone else in jail? We know the fear of daddy kept you from running. What about Cat?"

"Kennedi," I said. "Cat won't leave if she thinks Kennedi can't get away, too."

* * *

Lauren at least took some of my advice and put them in the wifey rotation that night. Cat got the big wifey night with Shorty and Kennedi got a little wifey night with Blade. And, yes, there was some grumbling by the girls whose wifey nights were bumped back. When Cat got back to the girls' house the next morning, Reyna asked how the date went.

"I barely even know Shorty. And then last night he made me take a shower with him and…"

Reyna cut her off before she finished. We knew what happened next without her telling us. Reyna asked about dinner and what they did after that. Dessert Factory. Ice skating. That means they probably went to Memorial City Mall. It could have been the Galleria, but why drive further if you didn't need to? Cat kept trying to avoid eye contact throughout the conversation and would give the shortest possible answers. Reyna brought the conversation around to how Shorty treated her while they were out. She asked what parts of the night were the best or most interesting.

After no reply from Cat, Reyna gave up on having a real conversation with her and left the room. I asked Cat what she thought about Shorty.

She finally shouted, "I don't know!" She took a breath. "Shorty's a fine upstanding guy who treated me like a princess, then made me have sex with him. Because that's what fine upstanding guys do."

Is sarcasm a step forward? I wanted to offer some comfort, so I reached out to hold her hand, but she jerked it away as if I was one of the bad guys.

Reyna had been trying to lessen the pain of Cat's trauma by getting her to focus on the positive aspects of the date. Something I would have done, too, even if Reyna hadn't. Then I wondered if, by doing that, I was defending this whole operation. Maybe I was turning into one of the bad guys. I didn't know anymore. It's that numbness.

I asked Cat if they scheduled any more wifey nights that week for her with the other guys. She said no. I was disappointed Lauren didn't take my advice on that. I knew what would happen next.

I was so much against the ambush method they used with me that I told Cat what to expect over the next couple of days. She nodded in acknowledgment.

"They said the guys would train me, starting this afternoon."

Now it was my turn to nod. Initiation. Training. There was no training in what they did to me. Maybe a better term is conditioning.

"At least you know in advance that it's coming," I told her. "Shorty and Blade came to me without warning. They held me down while I struggled to get away and took turns with me." Just saying it made my heart beat faster. I paused to catch my breath and let the flashback fade. Then I told her, "Showering afterward will make you feel better."

I think her eyes softened as if maybe I wasn't one of the bad guys after all.

"The next few days will be bad, then it eventually gets better. After your initiation or training or whatever they're calling it, come find me. I'll cry with you."

I debated whether to give her the warnings Kanya gave me the day I tried to run away. At the time, I wasn't sure the warning about getting sold to a gang was just an empty myth told to keep us girls in line, but after Sarah's experience, it certainly seemed real. I warned Cat and told her she needed to consider Kennedi in whatever she decided to do.

After that conversation, I found Bulldog and suggested they give Cat something to help her relax before giving her over to the guys. Maybe I was wrong that acceptance was the final step in coming to terms with this new life. I think I discovered another step: helping new girls move through the steps. Does that make me an accomplice?

* * *

Thursday, Reyna was ready to put both Cat and Kennedi to work, but as far as I knew, Kennedi had no training – or initiation or conditioning, or whatever they call it. Lauren wanted to wait until Kennedi was older, and she got into a heated discussion with Reyna about that. Reyna didn't see any reason Kennedi couldn't start seeing clients right away and was irritated that Lauren told the guys not to touch Kennedi yet. Lauren, despite losing her virginity at an early age, didn't like the idea of starting anyone earlier than high-school age.

"She's still a child," Lauren said sternly.

"So was I," Reyna answered.

The conversation took place in front of Kennedi and Cat.

Lauren put her foot down. Kennedi would not serve clients until she turned fourteen, which was a few months away. Reyna imitated Lauren's voice and said, "We ain't a charity," before walking off angrily, muttering about the cost of food and housing and the need to earn one's keep.

I found Kennedi rummaging through the cabinet under the bathroom sink. She was gathering the supplies to clean the bathroom. We hadn't seen her alter ego, Kandi, since Monday.

Cat – or Kitty – started working that night. Kennedi stayed with the guys until Lauren finished serving her small slate of clients and took Kennedi with her back to the house.

After we got back to the house, I went to Cat's room to cry with her, but she was already sobbing into Lexi's shoulder. Lexi told Cat she was proud of her.

Kennedi's sickness

Since Kennedi didn't have the late-night work that the rest of us had, she tended to wake up a bit earlier. Blade invited her to go jogging with him before the others awoke. The days were already hot by that time, but few of us could get out of bed when the outside temperature was still comfortable. However, with such odd schedules, that was the best time Blade had found for his daily runs through the neighborhood. After the first few days of Blade going into the girls' house to get her, Kennedi started meeting him on the front porch.

About two weeks after the twins came, I was cleaning the bathroom when Kennedi rushed in. I'd gotten used to having other girls in the bathroom with me, even occasionally one of the guys. With so many of us sharing a bathroom, it just makes sense to allow one to use the toilet while another is at the sink or taking a shower.

But Kennedi didn't come in to sit down. She leaned over the toilet. I grabbed the toilet brush that I'd left hanging over the bowl with the handle wedged between the seat and the rim of the bowl. Leaning over toilets more often occurred at night in our house, not in the morning. Kennedi's hair wasn't long enough to get in the way, or I would've held it back for her.

We've all either helped or been helped with that at one time or another.

Kennedi was nauseous for several days. At first, we thought it was something she ate. Then we thought it was a mild stomach bug and we all hoped we wouldn't catch it. The first time she threw up was on the morning run with Blade. When they got back to the house, Blade went out and brought back chicken soup from Chick-fil-a for Kennedi. The rest of us complained that he didn't buy lunch for us, too – I know, we were selfish – so Bulldog went out and brought back Chick-fil-a meals for all of us.

* * *

When Kennedi's nausea persisted for a few days, Lauren went to Walgreens to get medicine for her. A few minutes later, Reyna shouted for Nora to turn off the vacuum cleaner, then she called for Kennedi to come over.

"Lauren wants to talk to you."

That made my ears perk up. I didn't realize how much of a snoop I was until I lived with a bunch of girls. I didn't hear Lauren's side of the conversation. Only Kennedi's initial response of, "I don't know."

In response to something Lauren said, Kennedi said, "I remember I was at school and the teacher just took down the Valentine's Day decorations and I had to borrow a pad from someone."

After listening to Lauren again, she said, "Yeah, that's about right. Six weeks."

Lauren came back with nausea medicine and a pregnancy test kit. She explained to Kennedi what she needed to do, then sent her into the bathroom. A few minutes later, Kennedi came out and handed the test stick to Lauren.

Lauren responded with several choice words. Not for Kennedi but for whoever got her pregnant. "I told Blade and Shorty not to touch you until I said so. And Bulldog damn well knows not to."

Kennedi was still looking down when she explained, "It was probably one of my foster brothers."

Cat and Lexi were there to hear that.

"What do you mean, 'probably'?" Lauren asked.

Kennedi reached up to a tendril of hair near her temple and began twisting it with her fingers. She seemed to focus on Lauren's tummy when she spoke. "RayQuon and Liam would do stuff to me. Sometimes I tried to hide, but they would wait for me after I came out of the bathroom at night and pull me into their room." She looked at the floor and said more softly, "And they would do stuff."

Cat later told us that Liam was the biological son of the foster parents and RayQuon was a foster brother. They were both about Cat's age.

Lauren was about to say something when Kennedi continued. "They told me I was ugly and would never have a boyfriend and I should be grateful because they were the only boys who would ever be willing to touch me. And they said if I ever told anyone about what they did to me, they would kill me and leave me for the coyotes to eat."

Lexi and I looked at Cat. She whispered, "I didn't know."

Lexi moved beside Kennedi and put an arm around her. "You should have told us sooner. I know what that's like. I missed a period and was so worried I was pregnant. I didn't want to tell my mom, but I finally told my brother's girlfriend. She just laughed and called me a slut."

Lexi looked off into the distance as she continued, "She's the one who always got me drunk and got their friends to do stuff to me, too."

Lauren gave a heavy sigh, but Reyna snickered, which prompted more choice words from Lauren. "You think this is funny?"

"Your girl's not as pure as you thought," Reyna said with a sneer.

"She wasn't giving hand jobs on a school bus," Lauren retorted.

Lauren put her hand under Kennedi's chin and lifted it so that Kennedi was looking at her. "If I come across those boys, I'll rip their *manhood* off. It ain't right what they did to you, and it ain't right what they said. You're not ugly. Look at me. I'm no beauty queen. None of us are without our makeup."

Ouch. I don't mean to be arrogant, but I thought I was cute with or without makeup, at least when the occasional zit wasn't flaring up. Reyna could be a beauty queen without makeup. And Kanya looked pretty cute without makeup, although she looked like a kid. But I got Lauren's point.

"The makeup just hides my ugly," Kennedi said.

"Sweet Pea, the makeup just highlights what you already have."

Then Lauren looked at Lexi and back to Kennedi. "We take care of each other here. This is your safe space."

As long as we behave, I thought, remembering that Reyna almost sold Sarah to a gang.

Reyna asked Lauren, "Do you want me to take her to Yulia?"

Yulia and her husband ran a smoke shop that also sold a few black-market items. Yulia's husband was supposedly one of Lauren's former clients during a rocky point in their marriage. Kelly had said "supposedly" because she wasn't sure his status was really "former." She swore she'd seen him at one of the motels. One of the under-the-counter items that Yulia sold was roofies the seniors used to make us more cooperative. Lauren avoided cheap feel-good drugs smuggled from Mexico because they might be laced with fentanyl. That's also a reason she didn't like giving us drugs.

"The cartels put fentanyl in everything," Reyna once said. "And a dead girl don't make no money."

Yulia also sold abortion pills. She claimed that a family member in Europe supplied her with the pharmaceuticals. I'd never met Yulia or been to the shop, but the older girls sometimes mentioned her during warnings about not using condoms. The pills were expensive.

"I'll do it," Lauren responded to Reyna.

Lexi rode with Kennedi in the back seat of Quick Sadie and held Kennedi's hand. Lauren made sure Kennedi took the first pill before they left the shop and set a reminder for Kennedi to take the second one the next day. Lauren also had Kennedi stay with her in the master bedroom for the next couple of days so she could be closer to a bathroom. Interestingly, Blade seemed to visit the girls' house more than usual on those days.

Time to start

Kennedi's wifey nights had been limited to little wifey dates by Lauren's order. Her date events included a movie and video games with Blade, the Hermann Park Zoo with Shorty (that one started in the afternoon), and shopping at Town & Country City Center after a steak dinner with Bulldog. Before each date, the other girls took turns helping her with her makeup and choosing an outfit. She was getting better at walking in heels.

About a month into her stay, Reyna's big wifey night aligned with Kennedi's little wifey night and Reyna told Kennedi they would be going on a double date to a Lingering Scent concert in The Woodlands. I was jealous. I'd never been invited on a double date, and I'd never been to a concert, not even in my previous life. I guess I could have suggested either one, I just hadn't thought of it.

When we got back home after work the night of the double date, Kennedi wasn't home. Cat checked the house and found Reyna in her room. Reyna had switched dates with Kennedi who was at the guys' house with Blade on her first big wifey date. Lauren was pissed with Reyna for not clearing it with her.

Lauren said, "I made it pretty *damn* clear to everyone that she wasn't ready."

"Only by your standards!" Reyna replied. "She's not a virgin, and she got to choose between Shorty and Blade. So what's the problem?"

Lauren got in Reyna's face, almost nose-to-nose, and growled, "You don't make these big decisions without me!" I think I saw a little of Lauren's spittle hit Reyna's chin.

Reyna tensed up and I thought she was going to hit Lauren. But just then Bulldog came in and said, "Hey," breaking the tension.

Lauren stepped back from Reyna and said, "Come on," to Bulldog, quickly walking to her bedroom, with him following.

Lauren's irritation carried over to the next morning. She was extra noisy in the kitchen, slamming cabinet doors. Several of us, including Reyna, came out to see what was going on. Lauren slammed a cereal bowl on the counter and looked at Reyna. If the bowl hadn't been plastic, it would have broken.

"She's just a kid!" Lauren shouted.

Reyna calmly said, "She's a big girl now."

I couldn't tell if Reyna meant that now that Kennedi was a big girl, she could go on the big wifey nights, or if she became a big girl *because* of the big wifey night.

I suspect Lauren was disturbed not only because of the impact on young Kennedi but because Lauren realized she didn't have as much control over operations as she thought. When Kennedi returned to the girls' house with Blade after their late morning run, Lauren stopped her and asked, "Sweet Pea, are you okay?"

"About what?"

"Your wifey night."

Kennedi glanced across the kitchen at Blade who was pouring himself a cup of orange juice and smiled. "The concert was fun, but I only knew a few of the songs. It was my first ever concert."

"I meant, were you okay that it was a big wifey date instead of a little wifey date?" Lauren clarified.

Reyna was in the kitchen near Blade when she interjected, "Kennedi, Lauren wants to know how sex was with Blade." Reyna immediately covered Blade's ears with her hands to keep him from hearing the answer.

I was close enough to hear Kennedi quietly tell Lauren, "It wasn't bad like with RayQuan and Liam. Blade was nice." She looked directly at Blade and smiled her broad brace-filled smile before disappearing into the bathroom and turning on the shower.

Reyna removed her hands from Blade's ears and patted him on both shoulders before turning to Lauren. She said, "See, she's a big girl now. And when she starts working, that's more money for your retirement fund."

Lauren went to her bedroom without replying. At what age does a prostitute retire? I can't imagine clients paying for time with a wrinkled old woman.

Reyna gave a thumbs up to Blade. I hope Kennedi doesn't get a crush on him. Unless she's fine with sharing.

* * *

A couple of days later, Lauren came home with a FedEx box and dumped the contents on the kitchen table. It was a set of tools that she explained were orthodontist pliers. She pulled a couple of chairs out from the kitchen table and had Kennedi sit in one while she sat across from her, knee-to-knee. Several of us gathered around to see what was going on. Lauren ensured us she knew what she was doing because she'd watched several YouTube videos of the procedure. She made Kennedi stick her fingers in the corners of her mouth to stretch her lips open wider. Laney stood behind Lauren, facing Kennedi, and mimicked Kennedi's fingers-in-mouth action, which made Kennedi laugh. It made all of us laugh except Lauren. She turned around and give Laney the evil eye, which made us laugh more. After the interruption, Lauren resumed her role as amateur orthodontist. With a few twists and tugs of the different pliers on the brace mounts attached to Kennedi's teeth, Lauren removed her braces. I think Kennedi stared at herself in the mirror for ten minutes after that, practicing different smiles and other facial expressions. Lauren gave her a metal pick from the tool set to scrape off the brace adhesive residue.

The next day, Reyna took her to the guys' house for training. At least Kennedi knew what was coming. Thirteen-year-old Kennedi became eighteen-year-old Kandi the following Tuesday night. She embraced the name as if it was her superhero alter ego.

Several of us used other names for working. I was Alicia, Catalina was Kitty, and Delaney – whom we called Laney around the house – was Delilah on the job. She took on a whole different persona and sometimes referred to Delilah in the third person.

"Delilah does things I couldn't do," she explained.

I think Kennedi was doing that too. It was more than just pretending. I think it was a way of compartmentalizing the sex work from their personal lives. I wish I could compartmentalize things as they did, but Alicia was nothing more than an alternate name, not an alternate persona.

On our working nights, Blade frequently checked on Kennedi – Kandi – between clients. I suspect some of those visits weren't just for talking.

I just realized something as I'm writing this. Blade seemed to pay a lot more attention to thirteen-year-old Kennedi than to the other girls. Before Kennedi, it was Kanya. Does Blade have a thing for little girls and women who look like little girls? I bet Lauren doesn't know.

-Review Session Three-

"She was a child!" Amanda Butler practically yelled at Alia as she handed over the marked-up manuscript. She included an expletive that Alia heard frequently during her former life, but that she had never heard from Ms. Amanda.

Alia merely nodded and said, "I guess you're talking about Kennedi."

"Who can do that to a little girl?"

"Are you talking about our group or her foster brothers?"

Amanda exhaled heavily, producing a sound like a soft growl. "Both!"

"Most of the girls were abused before they came to our group. Our guys just continued it."

"Where were her parents? I mean, her foster parents?"

Alia shrugged. "Some people don't have good home lives."

"Alia, I want you to know most foster parents are good people. You only heard about the bad ones. Next Sunday at church, I'm going to introduce you to some foster families. Good ones that love their kids and don't neglect or abuse them."

She took a breath to calm down.

"I'm going to tell you something I haven't even told Ty yet. Henry and I are taking classes to be foster parents. We weren't planning to be parents-parents, but more like substitute parents. A couple in our Sunday School class told the group how they have a hard time getting away to mentally recharge because it's hard to find people who are certified to keep the kids overnight. They have to trade time with other foster families. Henry and I want to be able to step in and give the parents a break."

Alia nodded in acknowledgment. "That's a good mission."

"Now I wonder if we need to go all the way; to be full-time foster parents. It just seems like there are kids out there that need a real place to stay. With good people who will take care of them. I haven't said anything to Henry about it yet. I'm not sure he's ready for that."

I don't think that would have helped me, Alia thought. But what came out was, "I'm sure the system could use all the families they can get."

As Amanda took the next section of the manuscript from Alia's outstretched hand, she said, "Tell me about school, Alia. Are your teachers easier on you as you get closer to graduation?"

Unexpected Vacation

In May, Sarah revealed that she was pregnant. She had been taking tips for raw sex; that is, doing it without a condom. That was surprising because she was one of the girls who, like me, was tricked into the business and desperately wanted out. I would have thought she would be more likely than others to strictly enforce condom use to avoid the potential negative consequences of unprotected sex. I have this unlikely dream that somehow this whole thing will end, and I will go back to a normal life, one that didn't involve a baby. I assumed she had that dream too. And I assumed she was naïve about the raw sex and didn't properly consider the risks.

Sarah knew about the pregnancy for weeks before she told anyone. If she'd been nauseous, she hid it well. Lauren and Bulldog were furious. Lauren drove her to Yulia's shop for the black-market abortion pills. But while Lauren was talking to Yulia, Sarah snuck out and ran to a crisis pregnancy center around the corner. The center helps women and girls carry out their pregnancy to full term, and even finds housing for girls who are kicked out by parents who want them to get abortions. I wondered if Sarah got pregnant on purpose as a way of escape. Maybe she wasn't as naïve as I thought.

After hearing what she did, I considered getting pregnant myself. I could go to the crisis pregnancy center, and they would take care of me rather than send me back to my parents. Problem solved, right? But what happens after the baby is born? By then I would be eighteen. How long would they continue taking care of me? I went raw a few times, but I eventually chickened out of the pregnancy escape plan.

I had this movie playing in my head where I escaped and went back to my old school and the principal announced my return in his morning message over the public address system.

We want to welcome back Alia Khalifi after taking a year off to pursue her dream of becoming a prostitute. While she was away, she set a district record for the number of sexual encounters in the individual female division. If you see her in the hallways, be sure to congratulate her on such an outstanding achievement!

I also didn't think the world needed another unwanted baby.

* * *

Sarah's escape caused a big problem for us. Lauren and the other seniors had a quick meeting to discuss the possibility that Sarah would report us to the police. The meeting involved a lot of shouting and more foul language than usual.

We had to move out fast. The older girls knew this could happen because it had happened before. That's why we girls didn't have real furniture in our bedrooms, only mattresses, boxes, and folding tables. Faster to move out that way. Packing our personal stuff didn't take long as most of it was already stored in cardboard boxes. For me, it mostly involved putting my makeup in a box with my blow dryer and toiletries, then carrying my three boxes to one of the trucks. The biggest effort was packing the kitchen. We girls handled that while the guys gathered the mattresses, folding tables and stools, and dismantled Lauren's bed. It only took us an hour and a half to fill the trucks for the first trip. With that round, the bedrooms, bathrooms, and kitchen cabinets were empty.

We left some of the girls in the guys' house to pack up their kitchen while the rest of us hauled our first load to a metal-sided warehouse that had a faded sign that said, "EAR CRE K TILE". A letter "B" was sitting on the ground below the "EAR", leaning against the building. I looked around for a missing "E" but didn't see it. The building was in an industrial area, situated between an aging auto repair shop and a plumber's wholesale supply store. The former tile warehouse contained a workbench of tools and junk that looked to be left over from a house renovation project. Doors, used sinks, light fixtures, and several wooden planks. But there was still enough space for all our stuff.

After that first trip, the guys took us girls to their house to pack up as much as we could of their belongings while they loaded the rest of the furniture from the girls' house into their trucks. Their goal was to empty the girls' house before the police had a chance to investigate. It didn't take long to finish the girls' house.

We had ditched our clients that night and just concentrated on moving. It took the rest of that day and multiple trips to the warehouse to do both houses. Lauren was in a bad mood the whole time and made it clear over and over that Sarah was the cause of our trouble. Each time she made her complaint, she replaced Sarah's name with a different word or phrase that I can't print due to school guidelines. When everything from both houses was finally stored in the warehouse, Bulldog pulled his truck into the building and closed the overhead door on his way out. Lauren took the mail from the mailbox next to the street and got in the front passenger seat of the Quick Sadie. Bulldog drove. I rode with Shorty's group.

* * *

During trips to the warehouse, Reyna used her phone to search for temporary accommodations. By early evening, she had booked a large farmhouse on Airbnb for a week. The house was near Seguin, which is close to San Antonio and near the Guadalupe River where people like to float down on rafts and inner tubes. Bulldog said it was a good thing this happened before school let out and families started vacations, otherwise, we might have had a hard time finding such a nice place at the last minute. This was our vacation. We took two trucks and Lauren's Quick Sadie and got there shortly after midnight.

The house looked like a traditional farmhouse on the outside – at least, what I imagined a farmhouse would look like. It had a large front porch with four rocking chairs, two on each side of the front door. But the inside was quite modern. When we got in, we girls dropped our boxes of clothes in the living room and fanned out to check out the place. Our exhaustion from moving seemed to have been countered by the need to explore. One large room had a pool table with two pairs of bunk beds.

Kennedi called out, "I get a top bunk," almost as soon as she saw the room and before continuing the impromptu house tour.

I was checking out the pool table, racking up the balls, and taking practice shots when I heard squeals of laughter coming from another room. I followed the sounds through a large bedroom with a king-size bed to a humongous bathroom. It had the largest walk-in shower I'd ever seen with two shower heads in the ceiling and multiple water jets on the tiled walls. I saw clothes scattered all over the floor of the bathroom and Kanya, Lexi, Nora, and Kennedi taking a group shower. They were taking turns twisting various handles on the walls to find which ones controlled which shower feature.

Kennedi saw me and yelled out excitedly, "Allie, check this out! Water shoots out everywhere!"

Lexi added, "Come in, there's room for all of us!"

I stood there thinking I would rather take a shower by myself. But they didn't seem as interested in hygiene as in the novelty of the experience.

Nora stood at the entrance to the shower and said, "You can come in with your clothes on or off, but you're coming in."

I would rather not get my clothes wet, so I chose the second option. I don't understand why a family needs such a huge shower. Even if the husband and wife like to shower together, they wouldn't need that much space.

I sort of felt like we were getting away with something naughty. We girls were laughing and splashing water on each other. We had all seen each other naked, but never so many at once. It was weird in a funny way.

Lexi spotted Bulldog standing at the bathroom doorway carrying a couple of boxes and staring at us with his mouth open. He barely got out, "What the …?" when Lexi interrupted him.

"Bulldog! This place is amazing! Come in, come in."

"I'm just bringing my stuff to the bedroom." He backed away from the bathroom doorway and set the boxes on the bed.

Nora got out and ran up to him, dripping water all over the floor. She got behind him and began pushing him towards the shower. It helped that she was as tall as Bulldog and could leverage her height. Lexi got out and grabbed his arms to pull him in.

He yelled, "Wait! My phone and keys are in my pockets."

When Lauren found us, Bulldog was backed into a corner of the shower in his boxer shorts and T-shirt, while we batted at the streams of water to ensure he was entirely soaked.

She folded her arms across her chest and stated, "I've been unloading the food in the kitchen and here you are, in the shower with five naked girls."

We stifled our laughter but couldn't stop smiling – silent laughter – as we looked at each other and then at Lauren and Bulldog.

"It wasn't my choice!" he responded.

"Which one are you sleeping with tonight?" Lauren asked coldly.

Bulldog pointed at Lauren.

She stared at us for a moment before uncrossing her arms and holding out her hand to Bulldog. "Hand me your clothes. I'll hang them up to dry."

Before she left with Bulldog's wet clothes, she called back, "Be sure to use soap."

"Is she mad?" Kennedi asked.

"She's been mad all day," I said.

Bulldog replied, "Don't worry. I'll make sure she's happy by morning."

* * *

The vacation was a nice break after having had men forced upon me about 1,350 times.

The Intervention

The next day, we went tubing on the Guadalupe River a few miles from the farmhouse. Before we left the house, Lauren walked out of her bedroom wearing a pale blue bikini and an orange button-down blouse, left unbuttoned for the moment. She warned us about sunburn and made us all wear shirts. I couldn't believe it took me so many months to notice that she had a tattoo of a bulldog on her left butt cheek. I didn't have a swimsuit, nor did half of the girls, so a T-shirt and shorts were fine with us. I applied sunscreen to all my exposed parts but still burnt my knees a little.

At the inner tube rental stand, which stood in front of a large stack of inner tubes, a couple ahead of us in line appeared to be having a bad day. They looked to be in their early twenties. The man wore baggy dark blue swim trunks and a light blue button-down shirt that was left open and had the sleeves cut off. A faded black baseball cap covered his shaggy blonde hair.

The woman was thin and had straight brown hair that hung down past her shoulder blades. She wore an oversized yellow shirt that was long enough to cover the bottom of her swimsuit. We could see the hint of a dark green bikini underneath. Later in the river, her shirt shifted slightly and we saw that her swimsuit was actually blue.

Her companion said, "You've been wanting to do this, so I took time off for it. I could've made two hundred bucks today, so you'd better appreciate it."

The woman answered meekly, "I know you work hard. I do appreciate you bringing us here."

The man handed her a wad of cash and said, "Here. You pay for the tubes. I'm getting drinks from the store." He headed toward the convenience store adjacent to the tube rental stand.

As the woman began sorting and straightening out the money, a twenty fell to the ground. Nora picked it up and handed it back to her. That motion caught the attention of her man as he was about to enter the store.

"Dammit, Mary Kate!" he called sternly from across the parking lot. "I don't work hard for my money just to have you throw it away!"

She looked at the ground as she said, "I'm sorry."

After the guy walked into the store, Nora commented, "It sounds like someone woke up on the wrong side of the bed this morning."

"He does that a lot lately," Mary Kate replied.

Lauren asked, "Husband or boyfriend?"

"Boyfriend. We've been together about," she paused to think before continuing, "seven months."

"Does he have a good side?"

When Mary Kate shifted position, I thought I saw a very faint discoloration on her cheek and left upper arm like faded bruises.

As Lauren talked with her, we learned that her boyfriend Carl had helped her when she was coming off a bad breakup. It sounded like she didn't choose her men very well. They moved to the area for Carl's job, from a town called Corsicana, which is about three hours away. I remember stopping for gas in Corsicana last year when Bulldog brought me to Houston. Carl's redeeming quality was that he gave her a place to stay. From what we could tell, she either didn't work or didn't make enough money to support herself.

Lauren's good at getting a lot of information from people while sounding like a casual conversation. Mary Kate told her – us – that her mother died several years ago, her father became an alcoholic, and she thought it was better not to be around him. That led her to move in with her boyfriend before Carl.

"He cheated on me and didn't even care when I found out. We got into an argument, and he kicked me out. Carl took me in."

"I'm sorry to hear all that. I hope today gets better," Lauren ended as Mary Kate took her turn at the rental stand for her and Carl's inner tubes for floating on the river.

We watched the couple all afternoon as our group floated near them on the river. Their day didn't get any better. Carl seemed to blame her for every eddy that pulled them away from the main current of the river, for forgetting the insect repellant, for not reminding him to apply sunscreen, and for other things that were as much his fault as hers. We and the other river floaters also heard his complaints about her taking an evening waitressing job that prevented her from being home to prepare dinner.

A group of Texas State students enjoyed annoying Carl by occasionally pushing the couple towards the riverbank while apologizing for the "accidental" bump. If I didn't feel so bad for Mary Kate, I would have thought it was funny, too.

The college guys, however, didn't push away Nora and Kanya who had bumped into them. From that point on, the girls seemed to be part of the college guys' flotilla.

Blade tried to position himself in the current close to the college girls. We heard him first give compliments on things like their water shoes, hats, choice of soft drinks, and anything that might have the remotest aspect worthy of a mention. He was trying hard to engage in conversation. The girls ignored him until one finally told him plainly that they weren't interested.

Reyna slid off her tube and swam over to Blade, dragging her tube behind her with one arm. When she reached him, she let her tube go and held onto Blade with one hand on each of his knees and asked, "Blade, why are you hitting on these skanky girls when you've got us?"

The girls looked at her in dumbfounded amazement. Even more so when she kissed his right knee.

I paddled with my hands to move closer to Blade. When I reached him, I put a foot on his tube to keep us from drifting apart. "Yeah, Blade. You shouldn't be trying to pick up dates, it's my turn with you tonight."

They looked at me, then at each other.

"Besides," Reyna said, pausing to make eye contact with each girl, "they only *screw* frat boys as practice for *screwing* their professors for grades."

Three of the four girls all turned to the fourth. She looked at the others with indignation and stated, "It was a T.A., not a professor!"

I didn't know what a T.A. was, but I quietly chuckled anyway, and Reyna snort-laughed.

Blade looked at Reyna, and then me, and then at the college girls. "You're right. So many women, so little time. What was I thinking?"

He jumped off his tube and pulled me and Reyna together. Reyna kissed him on the mouth. I would have, too, but I would've flipped my tube over. He helped Reyna onto his tube and swam off to retrieve hers. After watching the snobs' expressions change to doubt about their assessment of Blade, I was pleased with my performance in assisting Reyna. She reached out to my tube with her foot and dug in to keep us together. She raised her hand, palm out, and I gave her a high five. Reyna usually doesn't go out of her way to help anyone, so I was a bit surprised at this show of support.

There I was, helping Blade look good in front of arrogant college girls, defending his honor. This was the guy who raped me seven months earlier, partly with Reyna's help. It must sound very foolish to say I had fun with people who abused me.

The college girls succeeded in keeping their distance from us for the rest of the river trip. They occasionally connected with the group of college guys, but I don't think they realized Kanya and Nora were with us.

By the time we walked in the hot sun with our tubes to the pickup point, turned them in, and walked down the road to our vehicles, our clothes were nearly dry. We didn't need to change before getting into the vehicles. Lauren came and stood between Blade's and Shorty's trucks and knocked on the windows to get them to lower them.

"I don't like what we've been seeing with that skinny girl and her loser boyfriend. We're going to follow them and see where they go."

"Why?" Shorty asked.

"We may have to do an intervention."

Blade gave a thumbs up and simply said, "Cool."

Shorty asked, "Is Bulldog on board with this?"

I was sitting behind Shorty, and I could see Reyna raise one eyebrow as she turned to Shorty. "Why do you need Bulldog's opinion? If Lauren says we do an intervention, then we do an intervention."

Shorty took a deep breath and said, "You're the boss."

Reyna nodded in satisfaction with Shorty's statement and after Lauren walked off, added, "Maybe this will finally take her mind off Sarah and the *fricking* move."

* * *

I thought we might have to follow Mary Kate and Carl to their home, but we ended up at a McDonald's, which was fine because most of us were hungry. Lauren sat where she could watch the couple. Back at the tube rental parking lot, she had said "may", so I assumed an intervention was not predetermined. She also didn't share with the larger group what she had in mind for an intervention or what would trigger her decision. I was at a different table and not privy to her plan, but all of us watched the couple.

I heard the boyfriend make snarky little remarks from the time they entered the restaurant. When a man opened the door to come out as they started in, Mary Kate stepped forward, but Carl held her back. "He's trying to come out, you can't just barge in."

At the ordering station, Mary Kate was taking longer to review the menu than Carl liked. "You've been to McDonald's a million times, why do you have to check the menu as if you've never seen it before?" He wasn't smiling as he said it.

I didn't think those were triggering enough.

After we were all seated with our food, Reyna asked all those of our party who had phones to get them out. She grabbed Nora's, said something that I couldn't hear, then walked up to Mary Kate.

Reyna held out Nora's phone to the young woman and said, "You left your phone on the counter." Reyna laid it on the table and walked away.

Carl slammed his fist on the table and said, "Dammit, Mary Kate! How can you leave your phone lying around like that? I paid good money for it, and you don't take care of it!"

Mary Kate looked confused and fearful at the same time. She reached behind to touch her phone in her back pocket. Even so, she responded, "I'm sorry." It sounded like a phrase she used almost automatically.

Nora then stood up and called out, "Has anyone seen a phone?"

Just then the phone in front of Mary Kate buzzed and the screen lit up with an incoming call. Nora looked back at Kanya and called out, "Found it!"

She walked up to Mary Kate and retrieved her phone, saying, "Thanks for finding it. I lose it all the time."

The whole restaurant watched the scene, but few noticed that Carl didn't apologize to Mary Kate for his outburst. Instead, he scolded Nora with, "You should be glad we're honest enough not to steal it."

Mary Kate retrieved her phone from her back pocket, looked at it as if confirming it was hers, and then slipped it back in. I noticed her phone case looked similar to Nora's. Reyna must have noticed that as well. Mary Kate kept her eyes down as if she was studying a French fry on her meal tray.

Once they finished eating, Mary Kate rose from the table and gathered up their trash while Carl started for the restroom. Our group stood up, too. Lauren told Bulldog to pull the Infiniti up to the door for a quick getaway and physically pushed him toward the door to emphasize the urgency.

As soon as Carl disappeared into the restroom, Lauren walked quickly to Mary Kate.

"I guess the bad day is still going," Lauren said as she placed her hand on Mary Kate's back and gently rubbed between her shoulder blades.

If Mary Kate was bothered by the intrusion on her personal space, she didn't show it. "It was supposed to be a fun day," she replied. She looked at the floor as she added, "But it was just like every other day."

"I've got something that'll make it better," Lauren said, shifting her hand to Mary Kate's elbow. "Come on, I'll show you."

Reyna held the door open as Lauren firmly but gently led Mary Kate by the elbow outside to the awaiting Infiniti, which had the back door behind the driver already open.

Lauren pointed to the back seat and said, "Go on, check it out."

Mary Kate looked at Lauren with wide eyes and raised eyebrows. Lauren merely smiled and nodded toward the open door. With a faint smile that quickly disappeared, Mary Kate bent down to look inside the SUV for whatever it was that might improve Carl's attitude. I may have been stupidly naïve about meeting an online guy who pretended to be my friend, but even I would have been skeptical of getting so close to a stranger's open car door. Mary Kate was the kind of person who wanted to avoid conflict so much that she would politely go along with a stranger's request rather than protest it. But maybe since we had been on the river with her for the afternoon, she thought of us as more than strangers.

Lauren slid Mary Kate's phone from her shorts pocket as she shoved her into the back seat. Mary Kate's small gasp of "Uhn" seemed more a sound of surprise than alarm.

Reyna ran to the other side and jumped in from the opposite door, sandwiching Mary Kate between her and Lauren, who climbed in after Mary Kate. Lauren handed the phone to Blade with orders to put it back on Mary Kate's table. With Bulldog at the wheel and Nora taking Lauren's place in the front passenger seat, they drove off before Lauren even had her door closed.

Mary Kate called out, "Hey!" leaning forward and twisting around to stare at me – or maybe at the door of the McDonald's – before Lauren got the car door closed.

Laney rode with us in Shorty's truck back to the farmhouse, not as rushed to leave as the group in Lauren's Quick Sadie. I'm not sure it was so much an intervention as it was a kidnapping. I doubt Mary Kate would have gotten in the car with a group of strangers on her own.

Nora told us Mary Kate began jerking and twisting her body in a panic as if she was trying to find a way out, all the while pinned between Lauren and Reyna in a moving car.

Reyna patted her right knee and said, "You're gonna be okay."

Lauren patted her left knee and told her, "You're a sweet girl. You deserve better than Carl."

According to Nora, she sort of calmed down, but her face was scrunched up for most of the ride with tears running down.

A few minutes into the drive she asked, "What are you going to do with me?"

Lauren told her, "Treat you better than your *a-hole* boyfriend."

* * *

"Well, that was exciting!" Laney exclaimed once we were on the highway. "Is that girl our prisoner or a guest or what?"

I had a pretty strong suspicion that the "what" involved a DollarFly tattoo.

Shorty's phone buzzed before anyone offered an opinion. Blade called to complain he was disappointed they didn't get to rough up Carl.

"What do you know about roughing up someone?" Shorty replied. "The most you do is wave your knife around and make crazy faces."

"It works. They always back down," Blade defended.

"Probably because they think you have mental issues," Laney said.

"Who said that?" Blade asked defensively.

I think I heard a chuckle from Blade's side of the call.

Shorty laughed out loud.

"Maybe I'll rough you up," Blade responded. I'm not sure if that was for Laney or Shorty.

Shorty ended the call as his laughter turned to a chuckle.

We passed Blade as he pulled into a supermarket parking lot, and we eventually caught up to the Quick Sadie on the highway so that we arrived at the house at the same time. Blade arrived about twenty minutes later with several cartons of Blue Bell ice cream and cases of Shiner Bock.

* * *

Most of us weren't in a hurry to change after seeing the ice cream, plus we were curious about the situation with Mary Kate. Kanya and Nora, however, went straight to the shower.

The rest of us gathered in the kitchen and dining area for ice cream. Blade's group also brought back all the fixings for sundaes and banana splits. Reyna enlisted Lexi and Cat to join her in an assembly line to dish up the desserts.

I looked around for Mary Kate. She and Lauren were on a sofa in the living room having a discussion. Mostly it was Lauren doing the discussing and Mary Kate just nodding. Kennedi brought Mary Kate a paper bowl with a banana split, complete with chocolate syrup, whipped cream, and a cherry on top. She was reluctant to take it, but Kennedi took one of Mary Kate's hands and put it under the bowl. I saw Lauren say something and then Mary Kate took the bowl.

I wondered what she would tell people if she got away. "They kidnapped me and made me eat ice cream."

* * *

Nora and Kanya emerged from their bedroom about an hour after we arrived back at the farmhouse. They totally missed the ice cream party, but they had on makeup and were dressed for going out. They had dates with the college guys. They went up to Lauren, who handed Nora the keys to the Infiniti. As the girls headed for the door, Lauren said, "I don't care how late you stay out, but be back by the morning or we'll hunt you down. And don't wreck my car! We need it tomorrow. If you drink a lot, I'd rather you stay over with those guys than drive drunk."

Before they closed the door behind them, Lauren added, "Call or text if you need a rescue."

Lauren followed them, opened the door that had just closed, and called out, "Have fun!"

Lauren had just turned twenty-eight and didn't look much older than the rest of us, but she sounded like a middle-aged mom. Well, not my mom. I think my parents would rather I risk death than stay over with guys.

* * *

Blade figured out how to connect his phone to the house audio system and blast his playlist throughout the whole house. It was an eclectic combination of hip-hop, country, and random rock hits from the past four decades. Shorty and Bulldog pushed the coffee table in the living room out of the way and pushed the sofas back. We girls spontaneously started dancing. Except for Miki, which was Lauren's new name for Mary Kate after briefly trying out her initials, "M.K." She sat on the sofa and watched until Kennedi stood in front of her and with her hands out and waited. After a few seconds, Miki reached up and took

Kennedi's hands and Kennedi pulled her to her feet. She finally joined the dance party.

She stiffened a bit when Bulldog took her hand at one of the country songs. When she realized he wasn't doing anything nefarious to her, she relaxed. It was obvious the dance steps didn't come naturally to her. I was like that on my first slow dance back at the girls' house a few months ago. With Bulldog's patient guidance, she eventually got the steps down. Lauren had Blade repeat the song so Miki could have a chance to dance the full song after stumbling through half of it earlier. In the end, she smiled.

Eventually, the seniors grabbed beers and went outside to the eight-person hot tub. They stripped down to the swimsuits they still wore under their clothes and got into the warm water. Blade and Miki followed them outside. We could see them through the large picture windows in the living room. Blade shed his outer clothes and sat in the tub with the seniors, but Miki sat on the edge next to Lauren with only her feet in the water.

Kennedi went out, stripped down to her underwear, and slid into the seat next to Blade, leaning her head on his shoulder. I went outside with a beer and sat on a patio chair, unsure whether the others even noticed me.

"Miki, a hot tub doesn't work if you only put your feet in," Lauren said. "You have to get all the way in for the full effect."

"I don't want to get my swimsuit wet again 'cause I need to use it for underwear tonight. I don't have any other clothes."

"I already had the girls lay out some clothes for you. By the way, you're in the bunk room with Kennedi," she nodded towards Kennedi, "and Allie," she nodded to me, "and…." She paused.

She looked at me and asked, "Allie, who else is in that bunk room?"

"Lexi."

"So, Miki, don't worry about getting wet. Come on in, we've got you covered."

Mary Kate – Miki – removed her oversized shirt and cut-off jean shorts and slid into the water. I contributed shorts to her donation pile. I'm kind of small, but I think even my shorts would be loose on her. Her ribs showed. We needed to feed her more ice cream.

Lauren got out and directed me to take her spot between Bulldog and Miki. The water was not as hot as I expected, which made sense for the hot weather. But the bubbles felt good. Lauren sat on the ledge behind Miki, one foot in the water on each side of her, and began to braid her hair.

Stuck With Us

When I woke up the next morning, I saw Nora and Kanya were back in their bedroom, and Lauren and Bulldog were gone. They went back to Houston to look at rental houses for us. The rest of us, including Miki, went to Six Flags. That meant eleven of us shared two vehicles, so the skinniest of us, which was Miki, Kanya, Cat, and me, had to squeeze into the back seat of Shorty's truck.

We stopped at Target on the way to Six Flags to buy clothes and toiletries for Miki. She is four years older than me and had to get her clothes from the children's department. That's how thin she was.

At the end of the night, Miki said the day was fun. She even admitted that she enjoyed last night's dance party.

On the way back to the farmhouse that night, she noted, "Eventually, I have to go back and Carl's gonna be pretty mad that I left without telling him."

As if leaving was her choice.

Shorty looked over at Reyna, who looked back at Mary Kate.

Reyna asked, "Miki, why would you want to go back to that *jerk*? He treated you like *crap*."

I was sitting next to Mary Kate, and I put my hand on her knee.

"Well, that's where I live, in his apartment," she replied.

"Sweety, now you live with us. We're taking you back to Houston with us in a few days."

"But Carl will look for me."

Shorty tried to stifle a chuckle. "Maybe. But he'll be looking in the wrong places. When Blade took your phone back to your table at McDonald's, he ran into Carl coming out of the restroom. He told Carl a guy came in and you hugged him then went outside with him. Blade told him y'all got into a silver Tacoma, saying something about going to Corsicana."

Shorty chuckled again at the recollection of the fake conversation.

"Oh, one more thing. Before Carl came out of the restroom, Blade wrote a note on a napkin and put it by your phone."

We waited for him to continue until finally, Kanya couldn't wait any longer. "What did the note say?"

"The note said, 'I had enough.'"

Mary Kate was quiet for several minutes. I assumed she was processing the idea that she was stuck with us. Then she asked, "Who was the guy?"

"What guy?" Shorty asked.

"The guy in the silver Tacoma."

Reyna looked back at Mary Kate and then at me. I think she was trying to decide if Mary Kate was serious or making a joke. "Uh, Miki, that story about meeting a guy...."

Shorty interrupted Reyna. "I think he was your old boyfriend. His name was something like Joel or Jeff or..."

"Justin? Was it Justin?"

"Yeah, that's it. Justin. He really missed you." I saw through the rearview mirror that Shorty was smiling.

"Justin was my boss at the coffee shop."

Reyna jumped in to prevent Shorty's joke from getting out of hand. "You work at a coffee shop?"

"I did until my birthday two weeks ago. I turned twenty-one. And that was the day Justin closed the shop for good because the Starbucks they built across the street took all our customers. Now I'm a waitress at Big T's Diner, but Carl's not happy about that."

"Well, Miki, I'm sure Justin missed you," Shorty said. "And that's why he was willing to take you to Corsicana."

Reyna poked Shorty's shoulder and whispered, "Stop."

"But Justin drives a green car," Mary Kate mused. "Maybe he borrowed his brother's truck. He does that when his car's in the shop."

After a few seconds of silence, perhaps trying to recall non-existent memories, she said, "I like when you call me Miki."

Ten minutes after that, she yawned and said, "You were joking about me going with Justin, weren't you? 'Cause I went to your house."

She fell asleep on Cat's shoulder on the way back.

* * *

The next day we used Miki's lack of belongings as an excuse to hit the outlet stores in San Marcos. That night at the vacation house was movie night, which morphed into a sing-along session. Miki may not be the brightest bulb in the lamp, but she could remember the words to a song after hearing it only a couple of times. And she had a good voice. I wish I could sing like her.

We girls felt compelled to use the hot tub each of the remaining nights as the last event before bedtime. It was our duty to make full use of all of the house's amenities. And since several of us still didn't have swimsuits, it was a clothing-optional event. I think we freaked out Miki with our exhibitionism. She still joined us, but always wore her bikini.

During one of the hot tub times, Nora complained that when she and Kanya hung out with the college boys at their rental house that night after tubing, the guys didn't pay as much attention to her that evening as they did on the river. She suspected her height had something to do with it.

Kanya said, "I told you not to wear heels."

"But they make me look good."

"They make you look tall," Kanya explained.

In heels, she's six-two or taller, well over the height of the average guy.

"I don't get it," Nora mused. "Most of my regulars are shorter than me. My height clearly doesn't bother them."

"Nora, your clients have a fetish," Reyna explained. "As I recall, you had previous experience with college guys, and they were glad I took you off their hands."

Nora scowled at Reyna over that comment. "They never complained in bed."

Both of Nora's parents were alcoholics, and she was pretty much left to her own affairs from an early age. She was embarrassed by them and spent as much time away from home as she could. She became the high school tramp, sleeping with any guy on a whim, often secretly staying overnight with her various partners to avoid her parents. When one of her older partners graduated and started going to the University of Houston, she followed him, moving from high school boys to college guys. One of Reyna's clients told her his brother was about to kick Nora out of his college apartment because he and his roommates were tired of her, and she was just mooching off them. She was seventeen when Reyna brought her in.

"Don't let Nora fool you," Kanya said. "She had a couple of horny guys following her around like puppies. Just not the guy she was most interested in."

"Rick was interested until that redhead that looks like Merida showed up."

"That was his girlfriend," Kanya explained to us. "Nora thinks she looks like that girl from the Disney movie."

Reyna leaned over to Nora and patted her knee. "I can get Blade to put on a college shirt and meet you later tonight with beer and pizza."

New House

On the fifth day of our vacation, Lauren called Reyna on their way back to us to say they'd found our new accommodations. Different houses in a different neighborhood on the western outskirts of Houston, but they had the same feel to them as the old houses and neighborhood. Fixer-uppers. The houses and the neighborhood. This time, our houses were back-to-back. After we moved in, the guys removed a section of the fence separating the two houses and laid concrete step stones across both backyards from one back patio to the other.

And of course, Miki came with us. She even helped us move in and became my roommate. I didn't try to warn her to get away as Reyna feared I would do with Cat and Kennedi when they first came. I actually agreed with the seniors that Miki was better off with us than with Carl, even if it meant doing sex work. Carl was the kind of guy I feared my father would force me to marry. And maybe enough of my soul had dripped away that I believed our work was fine for her. I'm now ashamed of myself for thinking that way. But when you're trapped in a box, it's hard to see other options. Miki needed help, but not our kind of help.

As I unpacked my boxes, I came across the little stuffed Elena penguin. I thought about her family that I was so envious of. That part of my life – my first life – seemed so long ago. And the idea of having a family like that seemed more remote than ever. For better or worse, the only family I now had was comprised of the people in these two houses, my fellow prostitutes and our handlers.

I put the penguin on Miki's bed. She needed a family, too.

* * *

In my bed that first night in the new house, my stomach started knotting up as I realized the break was over and we would have to start seeing clients again. The other girls, even the experienced ones, confessed to similar feelings. Only Reyna and Lauren seemed eager to resume operations.

* * *

I overheard a conversation among the seniors as we were moving into the new houses. Shorty commented that Miki looked so fragile, that he was afraid he might accidentally break her bones on a big wifey night. Lauren assured him that sex wouldn't cause a fracture. She was certain Miki and Carl were having sex and doubted he was gentle about it.

Nevertheless, Lauren didn't put Miki into service right away and Reyna surprisingly agreed. They both wanted to fatten her up to look less anorexic so clients wouldn't be fearful of breaking her as Shorty suggested. Besides, women with more curves get more repeat clients.

Lauren instructed the guys to make sure their wifey nights with Miki included desserts. It was probably not the healthiest way to gain weight.

* * *

Once Miki understood that our operation wasn't like the Liam Neeson movie she began to relax more. I think we may have been the first friends she had in years. The afternoon after her second wifey date – a big one with Bulldog – she sat down next to me on the sofa and asked me about date nights.

"I know I'll have to be a prostitute eventually."

I just nodded. I hated that word, but that's what we were. The other words – hooker, whore, ho – were even worse.

"Do you still do dates after that?" she asked.

We already told her we have dates – the wifey nights – with our guys every week. I don't know what she thought we were doing when two of us went out with the guys each night. Buying groceries?

Trying to gauge her attitude, I asked, "Do you want them to continue?"

We were sitting on the sofa in the living room. She looked down at her bony knees and smiled as she nodded. Then she looked up at me and said, "It felt like a honeymoon. Doug was real sweet and took it slow."

It was my turn to nod again. I understood exactly what she meant. And I hope she gets to have a real honeymoon someday with a guy who's not having sex with a different girl every few days.

After about six weeks, she'd gained eleven pounds and Reyna declared her ready for clients. At least she had six weeks longer than I had to become mentally prepared.

* * *

A few weeks into Miki's stay with us, she was in the bathroom and called out to me, "Allie, can you come here?"

I went to the bathroom, thinking maybe the bathroom was out of toilet paper or something.

She smiled as she said, "I'm having my period."

I don't usually call attention to that. I asked, "Do you need me to get you a tampon or pad?"

"Yes. But this is the second time since I've been here."

I mentally counted how many weeks it's been since we moved into the new house. It was more than two months. I had two periods since then, too.

"Yeah, that's about right," I told her, still not sure why she brought it up.

"I haven't had a period in months and then I had two since I've been here."

"Oh. Did you think you were pregnant? You should have told us."

"I knew I wasn't pregnant. I just don't have periods very often. Maybe three a year. But I've had two in two months. It's like I'm starting to be normal."

I smiled and went to get her a tampon and pad. I guess *normal* is relative. I would love to not have to bleed out every month.

Blade Joins the Business

We rotate among several motels throughout the week, supposedly so as not to draw attention to our activity. Some of the motel managers know what's going on. Maybe they all do but choose to ignore it. One of the motels, Royal Slumber Lodge, is run by a couple named Patel. There is nothing royal about it. We working girls never deal with the motel staff, only the seniors do that, so I'd never met Mr. or Mrs. Patel. Lauren said they looked to be in their fifties.

One night when we got back to the house after work, Blade came in with us. Usually, the guys just drop us off and go to their own house. He made a point to find Lauren.

"How'd it go?" Lauren asked with a grin.

"I think you got what you wanted," Blade answered.

Nora asked what we all wanted to ask, "What's that about?"

Lauren and the guys were making the usual arrangements at the front desk. They spread the room reservations among several names. The guys left and Lauren was finishing up the registration when Mrs. Patel shook a finger at her – Lauren mimicked Mrs. Patel in gestures and accent as she told the story – and said, "I know what you do and it's deplorable. You're probably spreading diseases all over my hotel with your illicit activity."

"We're just supplying a need, as you do with the hotel," Lauren responded. "And we use protection. So, don't worry about diseases."

"Does my husband visit your harlots?"

"Mrs. Patel, your husband is a respectable businessman. I don't think he would visit my girls while he's on duty."

That was a careful evasion of the question. Lauren didn't explicitly deny it.

Then Lauren – as Mrs. Patel – sighed and continued the tale in her Indian accent, "He has been in Oklahoma for several weeks, helping his cousin get a hotel going. The bank records show he got cash from an ATM. Who needs cash these days? Then I saw from his phone location that he has visited a hotel near the airport that has nothing to do with his cousin's hotel."

Lauren said he probably had a legitimate reason to go there. "I told her, 'Maybe he's checking out the competition or trying to recruit their staff.'"

Lauren gave up the accent but continued with Mrs. Patel's response. "I wish I could believe that, but he wouldn't need cash for recruiting. And I know he visited brothels in Amsterdam several years ago with his good-for-nothing brother. He was stupid enough to use his credit card and I monitor the transactions."

Lauren told her men get lonely when away from their wives.

"Do they think the wives don't get lonely, too? I'm working all the time. My son doesn't help enough because he spends so much time with his girlfriend. Why do wives do the work so men can enjoy themselves with women they are not married to?"

"Turn the tables," Lauren told her.

"What do you mean?"

"He's away. You're in charge. And you deserve a break from loneliness just as much as your husband."

Lauren said she scowled at her for a few seconds, then began writing room numbers on the little folders that she put the keycards into. When done, she gathered them up and held them out for Lauren.

Lauren asked, "Which of our rooms is closest to this office?"

"103."

"I'll take that room for myself. I leave at eleven tonight and after that, the room will be free. I'll have one of our guys wait there for you to… ah… ease your loneliness. Which guy do you prefer?"

Lauren said Mrs. Patel looked at her like she was crazy. After a few seconds of Mrs. Patel just staring at her, Lauren said, "I'll pick one," and opened the door to leave the office.

Just as Lauren stepped out, Mrs. Patel said, "The blonde boy." Lauren had used the accent again. She smiled slyly after that last imitation of Mrs. Patel and looked at Blade.

None of our guys fit my definition of blonde, but Blade has light brown hair, lighter than the others.

Blade took up the story from there. "When Lauren told me I had to show Mrs. Patel a good time, I thought she was joking. I've never been with anyone but the girls in our group. But before she went home," he waved his hand toward Lauren, "she made me stay in the room and wait. She told me if I didn't make Mrs. Patel feel special, we wouldn't be able to use this motel again. When I heard the door click, I half expected y'all to come in and yell, 'Gotcha!'"

Then he sighed. "But it was the Patel lady."

One of the girls asked, "How was it?"

"She's old and flabby! With a serious case of muffin top."

Another girl asked, "Did you show her a good time?"

"I had to. Lauren said we'd lose the motel if I didn't. But the whole time she wouldn't look me in the eye."

"What about you?"

"I powered through, but it wasn't pleasant. And her breath stinks."

"Welcome to our world," Reyna said. We all laughed except Blade.

Arrested

One Saturday night in late July some women from a church came to the motel and put goodie bags on the doors of our rooms. Somehow the church group knew which rooms we were in because other rooms that had regular guests didn't get bags. Kelly thinks they either bribed the front desk or staked out the motel before we arrived.

Each bag had candy, a package of baby wipes, ten condoms, a small Bible, and a pamphlet that said we were all sinners, but Jesus could save us from hell. Our guys watched the ladies distribute the bags, and they collected them as soon as the church group left. They gave them to us later and made us share the candy with them. I noticed all the items, including the bags, had a label or stamp with the church name and address. That is, all except the condoms. Do they not want our clients to know where their church is? Church-affiliated condoms would make for an interesting marketing campaign. I wonder how the group reported condom purchases in their church budget.

That was also the night we were arrested. Laney – she was working, so I should call her Delilah – thinks the church ladies called the cops after they left the bags, but Kanya said the church ladies left bags once before and the cops didn't come. It would defeat their ministry to us poor wretched souls. Delilah came up with a new theory that one of the church ladies went rogue and made the call without consulting the others.

This was the motel operated by the Patels. My theory is that Mrs. Patel did it to discourage us from using her motel again to prevent us from possibly telling Mr. Patel about her rendezvous with Blade.

The police arrested us girls and our clients. Shorty and Blade somehow got away. They don't park the trucks at the motel, they park at a business next door. So, when the police pulled into the parking lot, Shorty and Blade saw them coming and ran behind the building before the cops saw them. But Bulldog didn't get away. When the police came, he raised his hands, still holding the goodie bags he'd collected from the doors.

As we were being cuffed and stuffed into police vans, we saw the police just let Bulldog and Lauren go. Amazingly, they convinced the police they were from a church group distributing goodie bags to the poor prostitutes. Lauren made a big production of telling the police that "those poor prostitutes are victims of a broken society, and they need God." It was a good thing she was wearing one of her less slutty dresses, but I still can't believe the cops fell for it.

At the police station, I didn't see Kennedi or Nora. I saw all the other girls, but not them. None of us saw them in the police vans and just assumed they were in another vehicle. I feared that the police realized how young Kennedi was and took her separately to a juvenile jail. But that didn't explain why Nora was missing. Maybe she got away.

After a couple of hours at the downtown police station, they let us go. They dropped the charges, opened the doors, and just let us walk out. I had given them a fake name and birthdate – all of us did – and I thought for sure they would keep us in jail until they could find out who we really were. But no, they just let us go. I don't know if the police station always looked so busy or if it was just extra busy that night. Maybe they already had their quota of criminals and didn't need anymore. They kept our clients, though.

Before we left, a female officer told us they could help us get out of prostitution and she gave us each a card with the number of a sex trafficking hotline. I didn't even realize what we did was sex trafficking. I thought sex trafficking was about taking girls to other countries against their will to sell them to Arab Sultans or Malaysian billionaires or something like that. We were living in a house in the suburbs and had wifey date nights and Monday Funday. I mean, I knew it wasn't right, I just didn't think of it as sex trafficking.

Lauren and Shorty were waiting for us in the police station parking lot. Lauren told us that after the police took us away, Kennedi and Nora came out of their rooms. They had been between appointments at the time. Kennedi had grabbed her belongings and hid under the bed when she heard the police outside, so the police thought whoever was in the room had left. I was impressed that a thirteen-year-old was clever enough to grab her bag before hiding.

I was even more impressed with Nora. She had convinced the police that she was a regular guest of the motel. Upon hearing the noise outside, she quickly wrapped her hair in a towel, wrapped another towel around her body, and washed off her makeup. She told the police she was getting ready to go to sleep. I'm not sure the ruse will work if several of us use the same technique. How likely is it that several young single women stay in a cheap motel on the same night? I guess we could say we were attending a conference or something.

When we were getting out of the vehicles at the girls' house, Reyna held up her hotline card. "You can call this number if you want. But if you're under eighteen, they'll have to call CPS and you know what that means."

I didn't know what that meant. Lauren explained that they would put me in foster care and then call my parents. If CPS thought my parents had a safe environment, they would send me back to them. If not, they might put me in a group home run by creepy perverts. Or find a foster family for me. Some of the girls didn't have good experiences with foster homes, so that didn't seem like a good option. I didn't want to go back home. I mean, I wish I'd never left, but I didn't think home was a safe place anymore.

I knew what I was, but I was relieved that I wouldn't have a conviction to confirm it to the world. I admit that I cried a little in jail. Several of us did.

Miki seemed to take the arrest harder than anyone else. It happened just as she seemed to finally get over the morality barrier of being a prostitute, about three weeks into her new career. The arrest highlighted to her that what we did was not only morally repugnant but also criminal. We all knew that on an intellectual level but being taken to jail in handcuffs drives the concept home. It took a couple of weeks for most of us to get over the fear of another police raid, but Miki brought it up every night for weeks.

* * *

I had been sold about 1,900 times by the night of our arrest. The police had a chance to be heroes that night – to rescue minor girls who were too scared to admit their situation – and they blew it.

A bad night

At some point during the summer, I think I was starting to reverse the acceptance process. I had gotten numb to the physical part of the whole sex-with-strangers thing. For months, I suppressed the mental uneasiness and told myself this was just a job. A dirty job. Like cleaning fish. That worked for a while. The uneasiness may have started to surface again at the end of our vacation, but for both me and Miki it was more distinct after the arrest.

Sometimes my work was like being a sex therapist for sad old – and young – men who couldn't get a girlfriend, or sad old husbands whose wives' social media addiction got in the way of intimacy. Sometimes it was like being the prize, a living trophy, for someone celebrating an achievement. "I got a promotion! I'm going to get laid!" Sometimes it was like being artificial prey for arrogant men who thought paying for a girl to be submissive somehow proved their manhood. (Sorry, buddy, but if you can't get a woman through your own merits, you're not very manly.) But as much as I told myself it was just a job, there was always this little feeling that it wasn't right.

Some girls pretended to be a different person at night than they were during the day – an alter ego. Kitty vs. Catalina, Kandi vs. Kennedi, Delilah vs. Delaney. For me, Alicia was a different name but the same me. I thought that as my soul was eroded by all those little drips, I would feel less dirty. There were times when I would get drunk to try to feel better, and then later get mad at myself and avoid the alcohol for several days.

Or maybe my unsettled feeling started when Kennedi started working and I witnessed a child thrust into a business no child should be in.

Then Sarah left and we had to move suddenly. Granted, the time at the farmhouse was a welcome reprieve, but the move highlighted how precarious our living situation was.

Then we got arrested and the uneasiness moved up a notch or two on the uneasiness dial.

A few weeks after that, Reyna was beaten up pretty badly by a client. Shorty and Blade were on duty that night but were oblivious to what happened in the room until the client left. She was in the hospital for a couple of days and didn't work for several weeks.

We all went to the hospital the next day to see her. Her whole face was swollen and purple and her left wrist was in a brace. Her mouth was wired shut to keep her from moving her broken jaw. Shorty told the hospital staff her injuries were from an electric scooter accident.

"The *bastard* came in with a you're-just-a-ho attitude and then wanted to go raw and I refused," Reyna told us through wired teeth. "Especially not with his attitude, like he's so much better than me."

"Maybe you shouldn't talk right now," Shorty said.

I wasn't sure if he was concerned about her health or if the hospital staff might hear.

Reyna ignored him. "Of course, I wouldn't do it. He put on a condom, and I thought that was that. But as we were getting into it, I caught him taking it off."

Shorty said, "Shh," and patted her good arm.

She didn't shush.

"I pushed that *frogger* off and told him to get out."

I'm sure she used a more forceful voice in real life than she was using to tell us.

"The guy said he bought me to do things his girlfriend won't do and said, 'I'll be damned if I'm gonna let *an effing* ho tell me what I can and can't do!' He thinks he's better than us, but he's the one cheating on his girlfriend and paying for what she won't give him. Ha!"

Her 'ha' sound more like a cough, coming through her wired teeth.

And what was that claim that he *bought* her? If he visits a doctor for an injury, does he *buy* the doctor? When you hire someone for services, both sides must agree to those services. That's how commerce works.

He got more aggressive, and she tried to leave the room to run to Shorty or Blade. He caught her before she could open the door, lifted her into the air, and threw her onto the bed. He forced himself on her again and she began struggling and hitting him to get him off her. During the struggle, her menstrual cup slipped, and her period blood leaked out onto the bed and the guy's pants. We usually have no problem with the cups during a normal session. But who knows what could happen in that situation? That's when he punched her in the face, grabbed her wrist so she couldn't get away, and punched her again. Then she blacked out. When she came to, he was gone.

Most of us were at the motel that night and the client could have picked any of us. I felt a lump in my stomach, thinking about what she went through, what any of us might have gone through. Clients often got rough, but nothing even close to what Reyna went through. The other girls, even Reyna who had worked the streets, said they had never had an experience that bad. Miki and Laney were in tears as we left the hospital and I felt close to it.

* * *

The night after it happened Blade and Shorty disappeared. Bulldog was our lone protector that night. With Reyna's injury fresh on our minds and having only one of the guys at the motel, we were all uneasy. I kept picturing Reyna's purple swollen face. We asked Bulldog and Lauren where Blade and Shorty were. They said Shorty was at the hospital with Reyna and Blade needed time off because he felt guilty that he couldn't protect her.

Blade and Shorty came home late that night. They came to the girl's house because Bulldog was staying with us that night and they wanted to talk to him in person. I saw them when they came in. They were dirty and their shirts had red stains. Cat looked alarmed and asked if they were bleeding.

Shorty answered, "We're fine."

Blade added, "Sometimes you get dirty when taking out the trash."

Dirt isn't red.

Decline

When Reyna got out of the hospital, she stayed with Shorty in the guy's house behind ours. She was on a liquid diet since she couldn't open her mouth to chew. After the bruises healed enough that makeup could hide them, Reyna started seeing clients even with her jaw still wired shut. It was her choice. Shorty wanted her to wait. In the meantime, we made smoothies for her.

Mary Kate's emotional recovery was taking longer than Reyna's physical recovery. My attitude changes were mild compared to Mary Kate's. Her mental state was already in decline after the arrest. It took a dive after Reyna's attack.

In the first few months with us, she was cheerful, talking more, and often singing, even after she started working. Like the rest of us, she eventually accepted the fact that we got paid for sex and she settled into a new normal. The acceptance phase.

After the arrest, however, she became moody and less enthusiastic about life, and she didn't sing as much. It was like she got more tired by the end of the day. And that explained why she started sleeping later than before. I didn't think much of that because some of the other girls usually slept later than her and we all had days where we got more tired than usual.

But a few days after Reyna was attacked, Mary Kate stayed in bed long after everyone else. I had to drag her out to get lunch. Afterward, she went back to bed.

I thought maybe she had mono. Some of the kids back at my school in St. Louis got it and one of the symptoms was being tired. But Lauren pointed out that all of us were around her all the time and no one else was sick, not even the guys who were with her on wifey nights. Lauren had a good point.

It became harder to get her up and ready for work. For a while, I would sit her down at the makeup table, and then habit would take over and she would get herself ready. It's like she was a robot, going through the motions.

At one point, she just refused to cooperate. Blade got his cattle prod and zapped her with it to get her moving. It worked. It got her moving, but she cried the whole time. Nora grabbed the prod from Blade and zapped him with it. Shorty and Bulldog got between them to stop Blade from retaliating. Nora broke the cattle prod and threw the pieces on the floor at Blade's feet.

When Miki's clients complained that she wasn't doing anything other than lying in bed like a dead fish, the seniors finally relieved her of all motel work. Everyone gets depressed occasionally. But this had been a while and didn't seem to be getting better.

When I noticed Mary Kate had lost weight and her body started to revert to the emaciated condition of when we first met her, I told Lauren we should take her somewhere to get help. That led to an argument among the seniors about having to move again. From that argument, I learned that the last move cost them about $20,000 in paying out unused rent, lost revenue, new lease deposits, and the cost of our vacation house. And they were reluctant to spend another twenty grand so soon. Reyna mentioned the gangs, and Shorty and Lauren immediately said no, with a few colorful words for emphasis. For Mary Kate, it would be a death sentence. Even Reyna seemed ashamed for suggesting it. Unlike everyone's attitude toward Sarah, we all liked Mary Kate.

The seniors were stuck. They didn't know what to do about her without risking our exposure or having another expensive move. So, they didn't do anything. Except to keep her away from the motel and give her drugs.

She was withering away in front of my eyes. Since she was my roommate, I felt protective of her. If the concern about moving wasn't an issue, I thought maybe they could drop her off at a clinic or hospital or something. The question was how to get them over their concern. One way was if Mary Kate snuck out on her own. I tried to convince her to go and told her I would provide cover, but it was hard to get her motivated to take any action. She had previously expressed concern over where she would live if she didn't have us and didn't want to go back to Carl or her alcoholic father.

A second way was to take her to a clinic and trust her not to tell the authorities what we did, where we lived, or where we worked. It's not that Mary Kate wasn't trustworthy, it's that she wasn't smart enough to lie believably. Even if she didn't plan to tell anyone, she could likely let something slip, which would lead to more intense questioning and a potential police raid.

A third way to get the seniors over their concerns is if the group had to move anyway. Then they could drop her off at a hospital before she learned where we were moving.

Escape Plan

As I was doing my makeup the next afternoon, I remember looking over at Mary Kate lying on her bed, knowing she shouldn't be here, and thinking, *God, I don't want to be here either.*

Then this little voice inside said, *"Then don't be here."*

Can God be sarcastic?

That's when I decided I would have to be the one to leave, to trigger the move. Lauren and Bulldog had lived in an RV after they ran away. Maybe I could find a place like that.

One afternoon, I left the house and just started walking. I didn't take anything with me, no backpack or bag of clothes. I didn't know where I would go, just that I was getting away. Bulldog and Lauren were driving back from an errand when they spotted me walking along the main road about a mile from the house. They did a U-turn and pulled up next to me and Lauren lowered her window to ask me where I was going. I didn't have an answer. I just said I didn't know where I was going, I just needed to clear my head.

Lauren hopped out of the truck and opened the back door. She said, "There're other ways to clear your head. Get in."

I got in and they took me home. On the way, Lauren and Bulldog both scolded me about the dangers of a girl walking alone.

"Someone could snatch you," Bulldog cautioned.

It was broad daylight.

"You're part of our family," Lauren said. "If you disappeared, everyone would be upset. And the girls would remember you as the one who made us move again."

I got the feeling she suspected my walk was for more than trying to clear my head. But since I didn't have a bag of clothes with me, she couldn't be sure. I credit that with why I was spared a foot whipping.

At the house, I learned that Lauren's "other ways" involved weed and alcohol, which didn't do much for clearing my head. And they didn't solve the Mary Kate problem, either.

* * *

A few nights later, when we arrived at the motel, instead of going to my room, I snuck around the side. I wanted to go to the crisis pregnancy center even though I wasn't pregnant. Maybe if I explained the situation, they could find a place for me to live, as they do for the pregnant girls whose parents kicked them out.

Blade found me hiding behind the motel office. Lauren figured out that my earlier walk to clear my head was my first attempt to get away. I was afraid they would torture my feet again, but maybe because they were eager to put me to work that night, they found a different method. Shorty bent me over the bed in the motel room while Blade put a few stripes on my bare butt with his belt. Then they sent the next client in.

After that client, they made me take a roofie to get me through the rest of the night. And the next night. And the next.

* * *

Even with the roofies in my system, I would scope out the areas when we got to the motels each night. Some motels had more bushes in their landscaping than others. Those bushes may be a good place to hide. I took note of the vehicles parked around the motels. A lot of our clients drove pickup trucks. I noted which ones were already there when we arrived. They probably weren't our clients and might be there for the whole night. Clients don't stay long.

Some clients backed into the parking spaces right in front. It would be quick to escape my room and climb into the bed of a truck backed in like that. But the light from the breezeway also made it easy for someone to see what was in those truck beds. A truck parked head-in may be better for hiding. Away from the light, more shadows.

It was several days before I realized that the large toolboxes in some of the truck beds were hanging from the sides, not sitting on the floor of the bed. There was a gap between the toolbox and the floor, and some gaps were big enough to hide a petite girl.

I always switched up my outfits for work. Sometimes short dresses, sometimes shorts and a cropped top, sometimes miniskirt and a low-cut blouse. On the nights when I thought I had the best chance of escape, I dressed more casually, better for climbing and hiding.

I don't remember exactly what happened next. One Friday night in October I went to a motel with the group as usual; the next morning, I woke up in the guest room at John Jensen's house.

John said he found me wandering around a gas station late at night, not thinking straight, and he told his sister Sophie about it. She told him to bring me to their house. I don't remember any of that. I only remember waking up confused and a little scared. And hoping the seniors took Mary Kate to a hospital.

-The Final Review-

"Hi, Ms. Amanda," Alia greeted with a smile when Amanda Butler opened her front door.

"You seem more cheerful than usual," Amanda said, returning the smile. "I like that."

Amanda glanced down at the folder in Alia's hand, a familiar sight over the last couple of weeks, and her smile faded. "I thought we were done with your assignment," she said as she gave Alia her customary hug. "I'm not sure how much more I can take, reading about people abusing one of my favorite people."

Upon releasing Alia from the hug, Amanda added, "Remember you have to tell me something good before I read all the bad stuff."

"The good thing is that I'm turning in my paper tomorrow. So it's almost over. No more prostitutes and pimps and body counts."

"That's a relief. Then what's in the folder?"

Alia opened the folder and pulled out three sheets of paper, stapled in the upper left corner. "I want you to review the final paper before I turn it in.

She took the papers from Alia. "Is this the conclusion to that big ol' paper I've been editing?"

"Um...It's sort of a replacement and conclusion. I chickened out on turning in all the details of my life."

Amanda nodded. "Good. I was a little concerned about that stuff getting out in the wild. Kids can be kind of mean."

She led Alia to the dining room and then pointed her to the kitchen. "How about if I start reviewing, and you take care of the drinks? I'll take tea and you can get yourself whatever we have in the fridge."

A voice came from the hallway, "I'll take tea, as well."

"Sure thing, Mr. Henry," Alia replied. "I'll bring it to you."

Alia left a glass of tea on the table beside Amanda and then headed down the hall with another.

* * *

My Impactful Event
By Alia Jentler

<u>The Event</u>

The event was not a single thing, but a collection of events that started with a bad decision. Was it texting a stranger online? Was it meeting him at the mall? Was it leaving with him for a supposedly better life that didn't include a father who dictated who I could date and who I would marry? They are all connected.

To escape a life where someone else controlled my relationships, I ran away and fell into a life where someone else controlled my relationships. I had been sold for sex about 2,500 times by the time John Jensen found me. I blamed myself.

I had gotten so desensitized to everything that it took a while after my escape to recognize the depravity of my captors. I had stopped thinking of them as captors after I'd been with them for a few weeks. I had begun to believe what they had repeated, that we were just trying to get by with the resources available – our bodies. I buried the initial trauma deep within and eventually believed I was a willing participant.

It took several weeks of being out of that situation to realize how much they manipulated me into thinking I was one of them, shaping my thoughts to align with theirs, and that their way of living was the only option for a girl like me. Sophie once said it sounded like a cult. That's what it was, a cult without religion.

The Impacts

Nightmares of running and hiding from them.

One part of me wants to see some of the girls. I sort of miss them and still think of them as friends. But I also have a fear of white Infiniti QX80s. When I see one, I try to see if the driver is Lauren, from a safe distance. I'm afraid of being snatched like Mary Kate.

Feelings of insecurity, guilt, shame, and worthlessness.

When I was with them, I knew I could never return to my family. The shame of my life would forever taint that relationship, especially with my father. My shame stems not just from being a prostitute but thinking that I didn't try hard enough to escape early on. Was I a prostitute by choice? Ty Butler, John's brother-in-law, assures me it wasn't my fault, that I was brainwashed. But that doubt lingers.

Even if I could have somehow returned to my family, I wouldn't have been able to slide back into my old friend group. They would have inevitably found out what I'd been doing, and no one would ever look at me the same after learning I'd had sex thousands of times with hundreds of men.

When I finally did see my father, he made it very clear he didn't want me around him or my family or anyone else. My whole existence was an embarrassment to him.

That life is behind me, but some people can't get over it. Some see me as a prostitute who should be avoided or ostracized. Some see me as a slut who should be willing to fulfill their fantasies.

Then I met a convicted drug dealer who now teaches Sunday School to kindergarteners at John Jensen's church. She – yes, a woman – showed me that God's grace can cover my shame. I still have issues. I still have doubts. But I'm working through them, and things are getting better.

I now have friends who overlook my past, who see me for who I am now and who I am becoming. I even have a boyfriend. He is funny and sweet, and he knows what I was and likes me anyway. And no, I haven't had sex with him. Surprising, for a former prostitute, isn't it?

I love holding hands with him and I love the goodnight kiss that does not come with an expectation of more. I love dressing up for him. Maybe I dress up to compensate for the internal ugliness I still feel sometimes. A drunk guy once saw us together and commented that I was too good for him, that I was out of his league. That made me mad. I'm the one who was dirty inside. And he's like a diamond in the rough. That just makes me want to dress up for him more.

Stupid Questions

I generally don't tell people my background for the reasons I gave earlier, but word has leaked out. And those who don't avoid me ask stupid questions. I started keeping a list. Here are a few.

1. I know you didn't want to do that, but since you couldn't help it, did you enjoy it?
    What the heck! NO!

2. What was the sex like?

    What kind of question is that!? I wanted to say "screw you", but screwing is what hookers do, so I couldn't say that. I have to settle on calling them idiots. (But not to their faces.)

3. Why didn't you try harder to get away?

    Fear of getting beat up or sold to a gang who would keep me drugged up. Besides, where would I go? My previous runaway experience didn't work out very well.

4. Were you a drug addict?

    This is a reasonable question. Lots of sex trafficking victims are kept drugged up. But no. I went through minor withdrawal from the roofies they gave me in the last few days, but I don't count that as addiction.

5. Did they beat you every day?

    No. People can't understand why I would be willing to have sex with random strangers if they didn't beat me to make me do it. What do they mean by "be willing"? Don't they even think it through? Don't they realize that even if girls were beaten at first, they would eventually just go along to avoid the beatings? There are other ways of intimidation besides beatings.

6. Tell us about some of the men you had sex with.

    Fat, skinny, old, young, married, single, construction workers, accountants, cops, math teachers, truck drivers. Maybe your dad. What do you expect?

7. Was it really that bad, what with Monday Fundays and wifey dates and all?

That's my favorite comment because it's so ignorant. I have 2500 mental scars that tell me it was bad. If that kind of experience is okay with you, just post that request on your Instagram account and wait for the traffickers to contact you about a job opening.

8. Why don't you give speeches to warn about sex trafficking?

Because I don't like speaking in front of people. Because I don't want to keep thinking about that part of my life over and over, all the time. Because I don't want to be a professional victim. Because I don't want to answer stupid questions. Maybe someday I'll do it, but not now.

I'm being too hard on people. Most of those are not stupid questions. They come from curiosity born out of ignorance. I just felt like they were stupid at the time.

Believing that people only loved someone for what they could get out of them.

I don't think my father loved me or anyone else, for that matter. Maybe he wanted a son and resented me for not being one and resented my mom for not giving him one. The joke's on him, though. A baby's sex comes from the father, so it's his fault I'm a girl. But I know he hoped to get money by marrying me off to a stranger.

I thought I was falling in love with Doug. But he only saw me as a tool for profit.

Is love only a transaction?

However, John's family accepted me as someone worthy of rescue. They didn't ask anything in return. That guest room I woke up in that first morning is now my room. They accepted me into their family and love me like one of their own.

It was only a few days ago that I realized the people I live with aren't my host family, as a friend once called them. They're my foster family. I think of them as my adopted family, official or not. I even changed my last name to be a combination of Jensen and Butler. They are my family more than my biological family is and I don't know what they get out of the deal. Real love is not transactional.

* * *

I don't wish anyone to experience what happened to me. However, God can bring a good thing out of a bad experience.

Amanda stood up from the table, paper in hand, and walked down the hall to Henry's office, which used to be Ty's bedroom.

"What are you two gossiping about? I can't see Alia talking cars and fishing with you."

"She's just catching me up on life at Ty's house."

Amanda handed the paper to Alia. "Well, I'm done," she said. "I love it. You are one of the strongest people I know." That statement was accompanied by a hug.

Still hugging Alia, Amanda turned to her husband. "Henry, did you know she changed her last name?"

"Yeah, I vaguely recall Ty mentioning it last year. Combination of Butler and Jensen. She should have gone with Butsen. But she chose Jentler, instead." He then leaned toward Amanda and whispered, "Honey, you can let her go now."

Amanda released Alia from the hug.

"Alia," Henry continued, "that T-L-E-R part of your name is not just for Ty. Whether you planned it or not, that's us, too. Me, Amanda, Anna. The beauty of combining the names is you get a permanent reminder of the strength of both families helping you on your new path in life. You are proof that your past doesn't limit who you are and what your future holds. That's up to you."

Amanda pulled Alia in for another hug. "Alia Jentler, never forget how strong, loving, and amazing you are!"

Contacts

United States

National Human Trafficking Hotline
1-888-373-7888

National Center for Missing & Exploited Children
1-800-THE-LOST (1-800-843-5678)

Texas Counter-Trafficking Initiative
1-281-429-8888

Canada

Canadian Human Trafficking Hotline
1-833-900-1010

United Kingdom

Modern Slavery Helpline
08000 121 700

Australia

Australian Federal Police
131 AFP (131237)

Acknowledgments

I want to thank my wife for her review and feedback on the story and her encouragement for me to continue despite the dark nature of this subject.

I want to thank Cindy K. for her review of the manuscript and suggestions for improvement. I especially want to thank Cassie C. for pulling me back from the brink of publishing before the story was ready and pointing me in the right direction. I also credit Cassie for inspiring me to write this story. When she provided feedback for my earlier book, *The Gas Station Girl*, she said she wished I had told more of what happened to Alia before she was found.

The dark topic of what goes on during child sex trafficking was not a subject I was ready to take on, which is why I avoided it in that earlier book. When I decided to write her captivity story, I thought it would be a thirty-page short story. But the more I researched and the more I wrote, the more I realized there was too much to say to stop at thirty pages.

About the Author

Todd H. Davis is the father of three kids (two girls and a boy) who were older teenagers at the time of starting the Jensen Siblings series. He lives with his "smarter-than-me" wife in the Houston, Texas, suburb of Cypress, which is the setting for his novels.

Todd spent most of his life in the Houston area, except for the two years in Japan in his twenties, teaching English in churches in the Nagasaki area. While he was getting used to Asian culture, his wife, who had recently arrived in the US from China for studies, was getting used to American culture. They have spent the time since then getting used to each other.

You can contact him through his website:

www.toddhdavis.com